Chapter Prologue

"So, where the hell are we?"

"Can't rightly say," said Dr. Nigel White, his face pressed against the window. "There isn't much of a view."

In that, he was being generous. The window looked out into a light well, affording him a narrow panorama consisting of six vertical rows of windows. He couldn't see the ground, but if he turned his head just right, he could see the edge of the roof line. Above it towered the sides of two more buildings.

"Just windows," he sighed, straightening up and rubbing his neck.

"Shades down?" Asked his colleague, Dr. Philippe Nielsen, looking up from the pamphlet he was reading.

"No half-dressed ladies, if that's what you mean. And the windows immediately across from us are completely dark, in case you were thinking of sending out semaphore signals."

"And they'll probably move us before anybody comes in to work, you can bet on it," Phil grumbled. "Put us somewhere with no windows at all." He tossed the pamphlet back onto the table. It skidded across an assortment of other pamphlets, knocking the neat little piles askew.

"Nothing but bullshit."

They had found themselves in what looked like a two bed hospital ward furnished with the usual spartan symmetry: two beds, two chairs, two shelving units, and two little adjustable wheeled tables. The only thing without a double was the nurse's trolley parked just inside the door. It had appeared about an hour ago, along with an unusually reticent nurse. They hadn't been able to get her to say much beyond "you might be feeling a little woozy from the transfer," and "the Facilitator will be about shortly" as she served their breakfasts.

Considering what had been on the trays, she needn't have bothered coming in at all.

"Breakfast" turned out to be a thick porridge of unknown origin, a sliced pear, a pot of cream, and a small glass of apple juice. Nigel had eaten better on the aeroplane.

But he was too hungry to be picky and had downed the lot. Phil, on the other hand, could only manage the pear and juice, setting aside the porridge after only one taste. It sat there on his tray with the spoon still sticking out of it, perfectly upright.

Nigel's watch told him it was 9:00 am Chicago time, although from the light outside, it seemed earlier somehow. A trick of the light well, perhaps?

Still hungry and frustrated, (*Janice must be beside herself, wondering where we've got to*) he began looking through the pamphlets as well. They were the typical government boilerplate, full of cartoons of smiling people telling you about all the wonderful things bureaucratic regulation can bring to your life. Red tape naturally being the glue that holds

FACILITATORS

By

JOHANNA GEDRAITIS

ISBN-13: 978-1463685072

ISBN-10:   1463685076

Dedication:

To an Eensy Weensy Spider,

my mentor in Web publishing,

(not the one behind the sofa)

for helping me launch.

Pity about the curds and whey.

civilization together.

Granted, these weren't *quite* the usual. He'd never seen a brochure explaining how to use a lift before.

"Printed for the Vai-tock Liaison Office of Titan City," Nigel read. "So where is Titan City?"

"Search me," Phil answered. "What's a vai-tock?"

"We might not be in America, then?"

"I'm thinking Wisconsin, though we could be in Canada. Don't think we're too far away unless our friend, Port, took us a lot farther than it feels." He held up a pamphlet entitled, *Making the Most of Your Rations*. "It's always possible this is just a trick, you know. CIA or something like that."

Nigel didn't find that thought particularly comforting.

The two of them had shared rooms once before – at University, when Phil had taken a year abroad to study in London. Nearly a decade had passed since then, but their friendship had endured, despite the inconveniently large ocean that usually stood between them.

Phil had once attempted to bridge that gap by enlisting in the US Navy -- only to find himself deployed to the Pacific Fleet. Still, he had managed to return to England on a number of occasions since, whereas Nigel had only been to America one other time: to act as best man at Phil's wedding.

This time, he was in Chicago to attend a seminar. The keynote speaker was Dr. Glenn McInnis of the University of Texas, a renowned oncologist and someone Nigel admired greatly. When Phil's invitation reached him, he wasted no time in picking up the phone to accept, despite the cost of the transatlantic call.

And he'd brought Janice along, figuring she could keep Mrs. Nielsen company while they were at the conference. Happily, the two women had hit it off. In fact, they had gone out to the cinema that night, leaving the men behind. With nothing better to do, the two doctors had wandered down to the hotel lounge, where they met with a pharmaceutical salesman by the name of Port.

After that, the memories grew hazy. Mr. Port had said something to Phil about a new club opening near the Navy Pier and somehow they had all ended up in Mr. Port's Cadillac, driving off to ... here?

"Wonder what happened to him."

"Yeah," Phil agreed. "I've got a few questions to ask our Mr. Port. Did ya notice anything odd about him?"

"You mean aside from the eyes?"

"What about the eyes?"

"Unnatural shade of blue, more like glass than anything," Nigel said. "And the irises never focused. He was either blind or wearing some kind of lens. I suspect the latter, as blind men generally do not drive cars."

"Didn't notice that," Phil confessed. "I was talking about what happened in the car. Though you were riding shotgun, so you may have been out too soon to notice."

"Notice what?"

"We got gassed, right? With all of us in the car at the same time? Well, wouldn't you expect the guy *doing* the gassing to at least be wearing a gas mask, or making *some* effort to protect himself?"

"Sounds reasonable."

"But he wasn't. I saw him," Phil said, nervously pacing to the window and back. "Just sittin' there, humming along; completely unaffected while we were going off to lullaby land. That ain't natural."

"Perhaps he took some kind of antidote before hand."

"Maybe." Phil didn't sound too convinced. He started to say something else but he was interrupted by the sound of the door opening. In walked the subject of their conversation, his arms loaded with books and pocket-folders.

"Well, speak of the Devil!"

In truth, Mr. Port didn't look particularly devilish. Chartered accountant was more like it. He was of average height and build, with dark hair cut conservatively short. Last night, he'd been wearing the usual dull grey suit and tie, but now he was dressed in dark green trousers, and a bright, jade green jacket with ¾ sleeves that cut off at the elbow. He no longer wore a tie and his shirt was open at the neck, revealing a curious, star-shaped crystal pendant.

At least, it looked like a pendant. Upon closer examination, Nigel noticed there was no chain attached to it.

The points of the star curved directly into the base of the man's neck.

"Good morning. Doctor Nielsen, Doctor White," Mr. Port said, politely. "I trust you have recovered from the effects of the transfer?"

"Actually, now that you've come in, I'm feeling a major pain in the ass," Phil said. "Now what the hell is going on? And I don't care if it's CIA international state secret classified or whatever. I wanna know where we are and what it's gonna take to get us back home. You understand?"

"Of course, Doctor," said Mr. Port, coolly. "That is, after all, what orientation is about – answering questions. I have here your Newcomer folders with your identification and banking cards already activated, as well as a full set of ration booklets. I trust you've already had a chance to look over the other resources provided?"

"Stuff the hoo-ha, Port," Phil snapped. "'Cause I ain't buyin' it. Now, where are we and how do we get outta here?"

"You will not be leaving," Mr. Port said, matter-of-factly. "The transfer portal only works one way. You have been brought to a planet we call Latebra; to the city of Titan. As Newcomers, you will be provided employment and housing, plus a grocery allotment to get you started. Full citizenship will be granted after an eight year period. For now, though, we recognize it may take a while to fully adapt, hence the subsidies and reduced status."

Phil just stood there, open-mouthed, as Mr. Port placed the books and folders on top of the scattered pamphlets. Nigel picked up the folder bearing his name. It held an ID badge for Titan City Research Hospital, along with other important-looking cards and paperwork.

"Why us?" he asked.

"This planet hasn't proved to be quite the paradise we'd hoped for," explained Mr. Port. "Nearly everything – air, soil, fauna, and most of the vegetation – is toxic to the unenhanced human. A filtration dome protects the city and cleans the air. Water, of course, we treat in the usual manner. Food has proven to be the greater issue, however. A certain amount we can grow hydroponically, but little can be produced in quantity. Grains, in particular, are nearly impossible to grow in the amounts necessary for feeding a city. Therefore, nearly all of our bread must be imported from Earth."

"Whoa! Whoa! Whoa there, pal!" Phil interrupted. "I thought you said the trip was one-way only!"

"It is. But only for unenhanced humans. For vytoc*, different rules apply."

"And what in the bloody blue *hell* is a vytoc?"

"I am," said Mr. Port, pointing to the crystal in his neck. "On Latebra, we work as Facilitators, ensuring the survival of the human population."

"And you really expect us to believe we're on another

---

* Pronounced with a short "Y," as in "crystal."

planet? Come on! Humanity can't even get to the moon yet!"

Mr. Port did not respond to this. Instead, he turned back to Nigel, continuing on as though Phil had never spoken.

"There are a few native plants which we have found to be edible, among them the meschel bean, which is what your porridge was made from. Because it can be grown in the local soil, it's produced in quantity and is therefore quite cheap. Unfortunately, we have also found it, and other native foods, to be carcinogenic.

"Statistically, stomach cancer is the number one cause of death among humans on Latebra and recent advancements back on Earth have made treatment there far superior to what we have here. Therefore, we have brought you here to help better our oncology laboratory at Research Hospital. We are counting on you to help us find a cure for the cancers caused by eating meschel beans and other native foods."

Nigel looked Mr. Port coldly in the eye. He pulled a small velvet bag from his blazer pocket and shook a thin gold ring into his hand.

"Do you know what this is, Mr. Port?" He asked.

"A ring?"

"An *engagement* ring," said Nigel, his voice quivering ever so slightly. "As you damn well know, I had Janice with me, who is most likely near to death with worry, thanks to you. This was our holiday, as you *also* know. We were planning to stay through the weekend, do a little sightseeing, and I was going to be the hopeless romantic and propose ... somewhere romantic. And now -- thanks to you -- she's all alone in a strange country and thank God she had the aeroplane tickets or she'd really be in the lurch!"

"And what about Lara?" Phil added. "We've only been married two years, and now she's in the lurch too. And how's she supposed to pay the rent teaching Sunday School? She'll lose our home thanks to you!"

Mr. Port was unmoved.

"They looked to be capable women," he said. "I have every confidence they will manage. And as for you, there are plenty of women in Titan City. You will adapt."

Phil had been resisting the urge for some time. But now he could stand it no longer. He rounded a right hook at Mr. Port's nose.

Like lightening, the vytoc caught Phil's arm and sent the larger man hurtling onto the nearest bed.

"There will be no more of that, Doctor."

Nigel returned the ring to his pocket and picked up one of the books Mr. Port had left on the table. It was entitled, *Life Under the Dome: A Newcomer's Guide to Titan City.*

The look he gave Mr. Port was one of pure contempt.

"I'll be wishing to make a formal complaint," he said.

Chapter One

Three days after their orientation session, Phil found a maintenance gate and escaped the city's protective dome. Lucky for him, a maintenance team was working nearby and were able to get to him before he suffered any permanent damage. But though the experience nearly cost Phil his life, it did confirm that Mr. Port had not been lying about the planet's poisonous atmosphere. There would be no leaving Titan City.

Thus forced to accept their fate, the two doctors begrudgingly acquiesced to their new routines. Phil, in particular, did quite well. As the years went by, he gained renown for a new targeted chemotherapy for bone cancer, as well as an improved procedure for bone marrow transplants in children.

But he still held on to the belief that their stay in Titan City was only temporary, and lived as though he expected to find himself back in Chicago at any moment. A photograph of Lara sat in a prominent position on his computer terminal and his wedding ring remained firmly on his finger. And though he could well afford to "move up," he continued to reside in the tiny, one-bedroom apartment that Mr. Port had assigned to them the day they arrived. If anyone asked, he'd tell them he planned to move, eventually... someday.

He'd been saying it for eight years now.

Nigel, on the other hand, had done a little better at assimilating, having moved into better housing after only a year. The ring, once meant for Janice, now adorned the hand of another, and his work station was liberally cluttered with photographs of two small children.

So far, he hadn't had the same amount of success as Phil, but that was gradually beginning to change.

Over the last few years, he'd been focusing on Latebra's flora, particularly those plants deemed edible for human beings. His current interest was a grain known as kessil. Though inedible, it was grown in great quantities as a bio-fuel known as "kessilene." It powered the city's motorized vehicles and small machinery, though, for Titan's poorest citizens, it was considered rot-gut booze. A cheap high for the down and out.

Oddly enough, those who engaged in drinking the hazardous liquor were found to be 70% *less* likely to develop those cancers of the stomach and small intestine caused by eating native foods. It had taken Nigel the better part of three years to figure out why.

Flipping through his written notes, he attempted to call up the appropriate file on his computer. So far technology had been the biggest challenge to his research. Titanian computers were far more advanced than the huge, punchcard-eating things he had worked with back in London. With only a monitor and a keyboard, it was hard for him to conceive of it being a computer at all.

Most operations were performed with a small, wand-like device called a compustylus. Nigel had never quite gotten the hang of the thing.

In typical fashion, his attempts at accessing the main file were greeted with a sharp, accusatory tone as an error message appeared, telling him he was attempting to enter his password on more than one line. Cursing under his breath, he pointed the compustylus again at the screen and clicked.

"After eight years, I'd have thought you would have mastered that by now," said Dr. Spaulding, working at the adjoining station.

"Magic wands were never my strong suit," Nigel confessed, finally getting the pass codes correct on the fourth try.

At least with that out of the way, he could use the keyboard. By Titan standards, though, this was taking things the long way round. Dr. Spaulding and the others used a small, hand-held device to keep notes and to transfer data to the main files, but the compustylus' for the hand-helds were even smaller than the one for the main terminal. So Nigel kept to his pencil. It was the one stylus he could use with confidence.

"Having any success?" Phil asked, appearing at Nigel's shoulder.

"Nearly a full remission in Subject 37," he responded, happily. "And Subjects 32 and 35 look to be on their way. If things continue like they have been, we could be looking at a cure for standard mescheloid carcinoma within the year, though I wouldn't be breaking out the champagne just yet. So far, we have to catch it within the second stage for the treatment to be 100% effective."

"And you did this with kessil?" Phil raised an eyebrow. "But then, I suppose it's no worse than the ol' nitrogen-mustard back home. By the way, you get anything on Subject 56?"

"No. Should I have?"

"Probably not," Phil admitted. "But I was wondering if they might have given it to you by mistake. You really need to see this."

"Oh?" Nigel finished updating the last of his notes and pointed his compustylus at the screen to log out. Again, he got the error tone.

"Damnitall! I was never meant to be a conductor!"

"Why? Does it want you to transfer a Liszt?"

Grinning at Nigel's pained expression, Phil clicked his own stylus at the screen. In seconds, the error message disappeared, to be replaced by the notification that all files had been saved successfully and that the computer was beginning shutdown procedures.

"Thank you, Zorro."

"Any time, Nage. Now come over and see this. You won't believe it!"

"Subject 56?"

"Bingo!"

Phil's work station was across the room and Nigel fought back the pangs of memory he always suffered whenever he saw the single, faded photograph on his friend's monitor.

He wondered what Janice was doing these days.

"And now, ladies and gentlemen, Subject 56," Phil said, waving his stylus at the screen. "That, my friend, is a spleen."

"I'll take your word for it."

Indeed, the organ was so bloated and misshapen, it could have been mistaken for a stomach. Nigel understood now why Phil might have expected him to receive a sample.

"Strangest case of chronic myeloid leukaemia I have ever seen," Dr. Nielsen continued. "Subject was a vytasynene addict – ghost child, in fact – male... approximately 23 years of age."

"A bit aggressive for chronic, don't you think?" Nigel said, looking at the slide. "Or does vytasynene accelerate the growth? I had assumed it was a neurotoxin."

"It is," Phil agreed. "But it affects nearly every cell in the body, which is why withdrawal is terminal. For instance, check out this growth along the dorsal side. That is not a tumour."

"But that's impossible!"

"Nope. Somehow this guy managed to grow himself

an entirely new spleen. Which is why I'm diagnosing this as chronic rather than acute. He's been this way for some time and, to be honest, I'm wondering if it was really the leukaemia that killed him."

"Carlina once told me that vytasynene was originally developed to aid in organ transplants. Perhaps that has something to do with it?"

"Could be," Phil said, closing out of the file and telling the computer to shut down. For a man who hated all things Titan, he was quite adept with a compustylus.

"Wonder if I could get with her about this."

"Trying to invite yourself to dinner, are you?" Nigel kidded.

"If you don't think she'd mind," answered Phil, in mock supplication. In truth, Dr. Nielsen joined the Whites for dinner so often that he had begun giving Carlina his ration cards.

Around them, the laboratory was closing down for the day, and the two doctors joined in helping with the usual cleanup duties. They were about finished when Dr. Peris, the head of their department, came out from his office. The bustle died down as he raised a hand for attention.

"I've just been informed that a citywide lockdown is in effect," he told them. "Those of you living in outside towers are certainly welcome to stay until the all-clear. I would, however, warn anybody wishing to leave, that security personnel are out in force, so keep your identification visible. And, speaking of identification..."

He walked up to Dr. White and Dr. Nielsen, handing each of them a thick envelope. Inside was a bonus of ration booklets* as well as new ID badges.

"Congratulations, Doctors. Today, you are real Titanians!"

"So, what were we before?" cracked Phil. "Plastic?"

"This is going to take some getting used to," Nigel said, pinning his new badge onto his jacket. The new ID had a green border, much different from the day-glo orange of his Newcomer badge. "But I do thank you, very much."

"Don't know what we'd do without you," said Dr. Peris.

"Well, you're going to find out in about two seconds," Phil answered. "'Cause we'd better be going. Sounds like it's gonna take awhile to get home."

"You're sure you don't want to stay put until the all-clear?" Dr. Peris suddenly sounded worried.

Nigel understood why. The last two years had seen a growth in anti-vytoc activity in the city, and Dr. Nielsen was rumoured to be a part of it. The last thing Dr. Peris would want was for one of his best researchers to get caught in a security sweep.

---

*   In Titan City, the cost of food is always at a premium, and ration booklets are viewed as an employee benefit commensurate with health care and vacation pay. Positions offering food benefits are much sought after in Titan, as workers who get corporate rations eat rather better than the ones who don't.

But Phil seemed unconcerned.

"Let's see," he said. "An evening lollygagging around here with you guys, versus Carlina White's cooking. Gee...tough decision. Bye now!"

"If you're lucky, there might be some left by the time you get there." Dr. Peris grinned before becoming serious again. "Now, be careful. They say the guy they're looking for is full-Caucasian, so keep your nose down and don't give 'em any lip."

"Thank you, but lip is generally Phil's department," Nigel assured him. "Now, if you don't mind, I have a dinner guest to catch."

He left the laboratory, following the well-worn path to the lifts.

Nigel generally enjoyed walking along the hospital's corridors. Given that one hospital looks like any other from the inside, if he didn't pay too close attention to what was on the walls, he could imagine he was back in London, ambling down the halls of St. Mary's.

Admittedly, stepping outside effectively ended any fancies one might have of Earth. However, for Nigel, they ended a bit sooner: at the lift. There was just something that struck him as wrong about working in a laboratory on the 93rd floor, and then having to take the lift *up* two floors to reach the entrance.

Rounding a corner, he caught sight of Phil at the lifts,

chatting with a couple of nurses. Taking care that he hadn't been seen, Nigel ducked into a stairwell, leaping up the steps two at a time. At the 95th level, he walked back out into the hall, catching his breath just in time for the lift to open.

"What took you so long?" He asked, nonchalantly, as Phil stepped from the lift.

His friend responded with a hand gesture.

"Found out what the fuss is about," he added, as they continued on towards the lobby. "Seems somebody took a few pot shots at the Prefect after his big State of the City speech this afternoon."

"Anybody hurt?"

"What do you think? Guy's a Facilitator. Anyway, they're calling it an assassination, for want of a better word, and the big guns are out in force, roundin' up the usual suspects."

"Resistance?"

"Could be," Phil shrugged. "But they're bein' pretty stupid if it is. I mean, it's nothing but an empty gesture. After all, why bother shooting someone when you know the bullet won't do any harm. And, really, for what? A quick trip to an agro-colony, that's wha...sweet Jesus! Is this a party?"

The lobby of Research Hospital was a glass atrium three stories high and nearly the size of a football field in length. It contained, not only the reception desks and main waiting areas, but also the pharmacy, café, and a children's play area as well. At the moment, one would have to take all that on faith as nothing could be seen for the mass of people. Doctors and patients alike were milling around, elbow to elbow; impatiently marking time until the all-clear.

"Looks like someone hit the fire alert," Nigel commented, scanning the crowd.

He saw several people passing around portable net-phones. Nice to see them being kind enough to share. Such devices were strictly controlled; issued only to those who absolutely needed to be in contact with someone 24 hours a day. This illustrious group consisted of policemen, trauma surgeons, the coroner, fire brigade, and (oh yes!) obstetricians!

"Oi! Dr. Landries! Over here!"

A middle-aged man waved back and began forcing his way through the crowd in Nigel's direction. Dr. Landries had delivered both of the White's children.

He didn't even bother to ask. He just handed Nigel his net-phone.

"Tell her you're all right and going to be very late."

"That bad, is it?"

"They've got everything shut down: verticals, helix, the zonts, everything," he explained. "And you can be certain of finding a guard at every stairwell. So far, I've watched six people leave and they all came back within five minutes."

Phil gave a low whistle.

"All this for an assassination attempt?"

"Guess if the bullet hits, it's no longer just an attempt," said Dr. Landries, giving Nigel a very pointed look. "Word is the Cat's on the prowl and he's looking for a full-Caucasian. I would strongly suggest you stay here and wait it out."

"I have an alibi," Nigel said, punching his home contact number into the phone.

Full-Caucasian. It was a racial classification Nigel found irritating, though it did made a certain amount of sense in Titan City. London, had had its share of dark-skinned people, of course, what with all the colonials living there nowadays, but the majority of the population remained white. Even in Chicago, Caucasians dominated to the point of being largely taken for granted. In contrast, most Titanians were a mix of white and black, with the government recognizing "mulatto" as the majority race. Light-skinned people were a distinct minority and Nigel knew he stuck out like the proverbial sore thumb. Fortunately, race here meant nothing more than a classification, useful only as a means of identification. It wouldn't affect your employment or your social life. Certainly, his race had never bothered Carlina any. By marrying him she had, in a sense, become "white" as well, but in name only.

Ironically, the issue was moot for Dr. Nielsen, whose Haitian mother and Swedish father ensured that he was just as racially mixed as any Titanian. *He* fit right in!

The click of a communicator answering pulled Nigel out of his reverie.

"Hello, Darling?...Yes, I'm okay...no, just heard about it...terrible, I know...It's Dr. Landries' phone...yes, he's okay."

"And Dr. Nielsen's coming to dinner," Phil volunteered.

"What?...Oh, you heard that, did you...yes, he's fine...was with me all day...I'll be home just as soon as I can...love you too, Darling."

He handed the net-phone back to Dr. Landries.

"Her Highness as been assuaged. Thank you, very much."

"Any time, Doctor," said Dr. Landries. "And give my regards to Carlina. Tell her I'm running a two-for-one special on twins."

"Don't even suggest it," Nigel said in mock horror.

He waved the obstetrician good-bye and set off for what Titanians euphemistically call the out of doors. Phil tagged along in his wake.

To exit a tower in Titan City is to find yourself in the middle of a massive maze of concrete, glass, and steel. The City, itself, fit into a dome two miles in diameter; so the towers were built very close and very tall.

Everything is interconnected, with a dizzying array of ramps and walkways going in, out, around, and even through the towers. At every fifth level, wide concourses stretch between the buildings, forming pedestrian zones known as "flats."

Level 95 supported the city's largest flat, encompassing sections of twenty-two towers plus the walkways joining them together. Five stories above was the next flat, which helped to cut off any view one might have of the upper levels. It was no city for anyone suffering from claustrophobia or, for that matter, a fear of heights.

It had taken Nigel and Phil months to learn their way around. This was mainly because Titan was a profoundly three-dimensional city. Whereas, on Earth, one gets around by following the very two-dimensional grid of the street.

To illustrate: imagine a tourist in New York, desiring to see the view from the Empire State Building. First he must find the street-side entrance and then take the lift from there to the observation deck. Of course, when leaving, he must go straight down to the street again. No other option is available to him.

In contrast, should this tourist visit Titan, he would not only have to know where he was on the grid, but also *how high*, as the flats vary from level to level.

This three dimensional nature was reflected in the forms of public transportation available. Streetcars, known as "horizontals" or "zonts," circled the flats at every twentieth level, while large glass elevators, called "verticals," carried people straight up and down. Putting the two together was a bizarre looking train called the "helix," which wound its way through the city's core from level 10 to level 110. Phil liked to refer to it as the "rollercoaster" as it did look like something the vytoc might have stolen from an amusement park.

At the moment, though, none of these marvels of public transport were in operation. In fact, the normally busy flat was eerily empty. The only sign of life, the music coming from a nearby pub.

"Not even a cop," Phil commented, scanning the deserted plaza.

"Keep looking, then." Nigel said, pointing to a staircase. A man in a uniform coloured lime green and black was staring back at them.

"At least it's one of the regulars," Phil said. "But keep an eye out for the SS."

Nigel nodded. The Security Services were the city's political police, operating separately from the regular police force and controlled entirely by the Facilitators. They had about the same reputation as Hitler's infamous enforcers back on Earth.

They didn't have to walk far to attract attention.

"Hey, you!"

"Yes?" Nigel responded, politely, as a man dressed in jade green walked up to them.

"Show your ID."

Without a word the two doctors produced their new

identification cards.

The man in green barely looked at Phil, giving his ID the barest of passing glances. His interest was entirely with Nigel.

"You're a doctor?"

"Yes. I work in cancer research."

"Been out at all today?"

"Only for lunch," Nigel said, speaking quietly and taking care to remain calm. "I returned at 13 and was in the laboratory from then until 17. My supervisor can corroborate. His name is Dr. Brendan Peris with Research Hospital."

The man didn't appear too happy to hear this. He thrust back Nigel's ID with a curt "stay in sight" and continued on in the direction of the helix station.

"We ain't goin' that way," whispered Phil.

Instead they chose a route which brought them down a walkway leading right through the massive bulk of Tower 16. Wide as four city blocks and 256 stories high, this was Titan's largest tower and intermittent shopping mall, with several levels set aside as retail zones. Naturally, the stores they passed had already closed, and even the restaurants appeared empty.

"You there! Show ID!"

"Here we go again," Phil grumbled.

Indeed, they would have to show identification three more times as they made their way across town. It slowed their progress considerably.

Nearly an hour after leaving the hospital, they arrived at a walkway overlooking Tower 22, where Nigel and his family lived on the 86th floor. From here, they could see the windows of his flat – or rather, his apartment. Titanians generally laughed whenever the Englishman referred to his home as a "flat."

And now, there was just that one last little problem...

"Jesus! That's a long way down," muttered Phil to nobody in particular.

"Would hate to have to fight that crowd again," said Nigel. "But the interior lifts were unguarded and working. We could always go back and try coming up from the Medical School entrance."

"Except that's on 75. Don't know about you, but I'd rather go down ten floors than up."

"Point taken."

"We could try a maintenance vertical," Phil offered.

"Wouldn't they be shut down as well?"

"Not necessarily. The police use 'em, so they're usually kept running even when the rest of the City's on shutdown. Could be guarded, but it's worth a try."

With nothing to lose but time, the two doctors made their way into the nearest maintenance zone. This was an odoriferous area, populated only by those whose job it was to sort rubbish for recycling, wash windows, or run street sweeping machinery.

They moved cautiously, but found nothing in front of the service lift but a little ball of fuzz.

The fuzz belonged to a deceased domecock, a native creature looking somewhat like a cross between a bird and a bat. They liked to nest in the dome's filtration systems and sometimes managed to find their way into the city itself. Such an accomplishment generally proved fatal, however, as domecocks could no more live in a terrestrial atmosphere than a human could survive unprotected in Latebra's badlands.

"These things never cease to amaze me," Phil said, nudging at the lump of fuzz with his shoe. "We gotta be, what, half a mile in?"

"I've heard some have been known to survive two days or more."

"And to think, I about packed it in after only thirty minutes. Maybe it's the smaller lung capacity."

A sound from the lift made them duck for cover behind the recycling bins. Together, they breathed a sigh of relief as the doors opened to reveal nothing more sinister than a street sweeper.

The operator didn't even look their way as the machine chugged past, taking the mortal remains of the domecock along with it.

"Everything's stopped but the cleaning crew," Phil said wryly, catching the door to the lift.

Nigel followed him in, entering level 85 on the destination keypad.

The doors slid closed.

But the lift seemed disinclined to move.

The doors opened up again.

A tall, blonde man in a jade green uniform stepped inside. The crystal at his neck glistened in the fluorescent lighting.

The doors closed again.

Nigel felt a chill go down his spine as he felt the lift go down a short way, coming to an abrupt halt between floors.

"Don't suppose you'd mind answering a few questions while we're here," said the Cat, smiling.

Chapter Two

I'm standing here on the level 98 Periphery maintenance bridge near Tower 6. Police think this is where the gunman stood before rappelling an unknown distance, likely to flat 95. Police are therefore focusing their search here, although it is possible the suspect could be lower down.

Jan, the assassin is described as a full-Caucasian male with sand-coloured hair. Do they think this could be Daniel Cawthorn?

Well, Mitch, we've been getting contradictory information in that regards. Security Services have both confirmed and denied that Cawthorn is a suspect. We'll have to wait and see as this develops.

Daniel Cawthorn, of course, still on the run after the murder of Cassandra Manning three years ago...

Carlina White froze at the mention of her sister's name.

Thankfully, it was only in passing. The newsreader was more interested in the search for Cassi's former boyfriend. She turned back to her cooking, trying to ignore the prattle of the television and the looming face of the clock above the stove.

We've just received word: Security Services have announced they have ended the shutdown. All trains and verticals should be back in service. I repeat, the shutdown has ended.

Does this mean a suspect has been apprehended?

No word on that, Mitch, but we'll keep you posted.

Thanks, Jan. Meanwhile, the Prefect has scheduled a televised address to be broadcast on all channels at 18 hours. "Moons of Tillyn" will therefore be shown later this evening at...

"Of all the stinkin' rats!" Came a whine from the living room. "Sis? Didcha hear that? They've knocked down *Moons of Tillyn!*"

"So, there's a chance you'll get that theme done tonight?"

"Not funny, Sis."

A young woman stomped into the kitchen to fling herself dramatically against the side of the doorway. Dark eyes framed in lavender eyeshadow gazed longingly up at the clock.

"Snurrgles! It's only a freechen half-section! Is he crawling home? I'm starved!"

"Christina, there's no need for that," said Carlina, the irritation in her voice covering for worry. "They've been on shutdown for two hours and the worst of it was on 95. He's probably having to wait it out."

"Or got caught."

"Christina!"

"Allrightallrightallright! But he's taking his damn sweet time....Hey there sport!"

This last comment was directed at a little boy, evidently curious to see what in the kitchen was so interesting that it could separate his aunt from the television. His spaniel eyes looked up at the women, pleadingly.

"Wa' Kooki?"

"No, Robyn. It's too close to dinnertime."

"Wa' Kooki!"

"You'll get a cookie later," Christina assured the toddler, hoping to cut off the temper tantrum before it started. "I know! How about we go play with Kitti! Ooh, look! There he is! There's Kitti! Go get 'em!"

"Kitti" was two-year-old Robyn's favourite toy. Basically a ball of fluff on castors, Kitti had big plastic eyes, a fluffy, dust-mop tail, and a cord for pulling. Drink enough kessilene and it might begin to look like a cat.

The diversion successful, Carlina was able to return to her cooking. Meanwhile, Christina returned to the news while Robyn happily sent Kitti rampaging through the latest block city.

At least the noise was drowning out the television.

Now for the spaghetti.

Semolina was extremely hard to come by in Titan City and pasta was seldom seen outside of the more exclusive restaurants. Carlina would never have bought it for herself. This box she had received from one of Cassandra's old friends.

She could only guess at how to prepare it.

"Genuine Italian spaghetti," Mr. Géricault had bragged. Unfortunately, that also meant "genuine Italian directions"as well. Anyway, Carlina assumed the language was Italian. It wasn't English or Dutch, the languages spoken in Titan City.

Spaghetti appeared to be a type of noodle. Well then, she would cook it like noodles and hope for the best.

There came a loud crash from the living room, followed by a wail of indignation.

"What's going on in there?"

"It's all right," Christina said from the block pile.

"Sophie just threw the video-wand at Robbie."

"She *threw* it?"

"Yeah! And she had to reach over the back of the sofa to get it, too."

Carlina rubbed her forehead, quietly counting to ten.

There are times when a mother doesn't know if she should jump up and down in celebration or just hit her head against a wall. Right now the wall seemed a good option.

Sophia was fifteen months old, but lagged far behind other children her age, having been born with a condition Titanians call "mongloidy."* The little girl had only recently learned how to sit up. That she could throw something (particularly something as heavy as the video wand) was a major accomplishment. That she would use her new found skill to attack her brother was...well...pure little sister.

"Give her some pillows to play with," Carlina suggested with a sigh. "And from now on, keep the wand on the bookcase."

"Un-derstood!"

And now, back to dinner (again!) and Nigel *still* wasn't home yet. At this rate, he might very well find himself with nothing but cold leftovers to eat.

She forced herself to put things in perspective. It could always be worse. If she were still working full time, she'd be

---

* Otherwise known as Down's Syndrome. It should be noted here that, due to a political dispute between certain vytoc, the Asian population of Latebra numbers zero. The average Titanian has no idea where Mongolia is, nor what the people there look like, nor why any of this should be associated with a genetic disorder.

stuck in the pharmacy right now and unable to get to her children, let alone cook dinner.

But a full day's tuition for both Billy Goat Preschool and The Titan Center for Special Needs proved far beyond the family's ability to pay. So, the children went for only half-days, Carlina picking them up after lunch.

Things had gotten a little easier now that Christina was in college. Aunt Chrissi had organized her schedule to allow for her to babysit Wednesday and Friday afternoons. The arrangement enabled Carlina to work full time for at least two days a week and reclaim her supervisor position. In turn, the White's paid Christina's activity fees and kept her fed.

Though she just might want to risk the cafeteria tonight.

A sample strand of spaghetti felt soft but Carlina was unsure if it was truly done or not. She wished Nigel were here. He'd know.

Best not to dwell on it.

Turning her attention to the sauce, it looked done as well, but perhaps a little bland. She grabbed her trimmers and went over to her hydroponic garden for a few sprigs of oregano and basil.

Most apartments in Titan City came with such gardens, usually positioned in the windows nearest the kitchen. Carlina's garden contained, not only herbs, but beans, tomatoes, and three kinds of squash as well. The many plants made for a green drapery that nearly surrounded the family dining table. Nigel liked to joke that they ate in the "jungle room."

Nigel!

Though she had been straining her ears to hear it, the sound of the door opening nearly made her jump out of her shoes.

It was followed by the usual rumpus.

"He's home!"

"DADEE!"

"'Allo, sport!"

"Guess what, Dr. White! I got Lynessa in *Wider Horizons*!"

"That's what? Third washer-woman on the left?"

"C'mon! It's the LEAD ROLE!"

"Oh, well good show then. What's for dinner?"

"You're not gonna like it!"

"What am I not gonna like?"

This last sentence was directed at Carlina as by now Nigel had reached the kitchen. Christina followed close behind with Sophia, while Robyn was draped across his shoulders like an old shawl.

"Sketti!" The boy squealed.

Carlina pulled up a forkful of pasta and, with some difficulty, separated a strand.

"It's flexible, but I'm not quite sure if it's done or not," she said.

Nigel gave both her and the spaghetti a disapproving look, but he went ahead and tasted the strand.

"I'd say it's ready. Don't suppose I want to know how you came by getting it?"

"By your tone of voice, I'd say you've already guessed."

"You know, you don't have to accept every gift he gives you."

"It's polite," Carlina said with the firmness of someone who doesn't want to fight about it. "Now, how about helping Chris with the children so we can eat."

Nigel rolled Robyn off his shoulder and into the booster seat clamped onto one of the dining room chairs. Christina did her bit by settling Sophia into the high-chair. By the time both children were strapped in, the spaghetti was on the table.

"So, what happened to Phil?" Christina asked as the plates went round.

"Said he needed to get with someone and ran off. Mind you, whoever it was, he likely led the jade brigade straight to them."

"The police were chasing him?" Christina was enthralled.

"Not the police as such, no," Nigel explained. "We were stopped by one of the blonder members of the constabulary and forced to answer some rather pointed questions."

"You were questioned by the Cat?" Christina's eyes were like saucers.

"It wasn't much of an inquisition, at least compared with the stories you hear. He was concerned there might be a resistance cell operating out of the hospital. Scared the whullups out of Phil, so there might be something to it."

"Phil Nielsen, the next Vyn Tyler," Christina squealed in delight. "Top floor!"

Nigel found that rather amusing.

"Somehow, I cannot see our Dr. Nielsen holding the entire City Council at gunpoint, while demanding that the Prefect sign his Accords," he said.

"So, maybe he'll do something different," said Christina in Phil's defence.

"Something effective, perchance?"

"Aw, come on. Tyler tamed the vytoc."

"Only to run off and start his own separate city," countered Nigel. "And from the look of things around here, I'd say the Facilitators weren't so much tamed as briefly subdued."

"I was only six at the time, but mother used to tell us stories," Carlina said, joining in as she fed Sophia. "Before Tyler, the vytoc ran everything -- no humans on the Council at all. At least The Accords changed all that; put the government in human hands. And there's only a handful of vytoc around now, not like the hundreds you used to see. But part of the compromise was that Tyler and his followers would go and live in exile in the Old Colony, which was abandoned once Titan was built."

"And a few tockers stayed on as Facilitators," added Christina. "So we can still get bread and stuff. But they're not allowed to mess with the government any more."

"So Tyler gets a fresh start in a vytoc-free city without actually liberating the city he started out in, and still comes out a hero," Nigel mused. "You have to hand it to the vytoc, they're quite clever. Though I seriously doubt they're as tame as some would profess." He held up a forkful of spaghetti, giving Carlina a pointed look.

"He was just being nice."

"Poppycock!"

"He was very close to Cassandra," Carlina said, wearily, having been through this argument many times before. "And he never got over her death. We are, after all, so much more fragile than they are. I mean, shoot one of them in the head and it only annoys them. Shoot one of us..."

Her words died away as she realized she had been gesticulating wildly with Sophia's spoon. The little girl was looking up at it, mouth agape, like a baby bird.

"Besides," she added, giving Sophia the spoon and trying not to look at Robyn, whose entire face was painted red with tomato sauce. "There was never anything between us. Maybe he's just watching out for me in her memory."

Nigel gave a snort.

"Darling, if there is one thing I've learned living in this oversized terrarium," he said. "It's that Facilitators never do a good deed without asking for something in return."

Carlina kept her mouth shut, wishing desperately for the subject to change. She didn't like to admit that Mr. Géricault's attentions made her nervous, not to mention all those curious looks she got every time he showed up at the pharmacy. She had no interest in being a Facilitator's lackey, but you couldn't say "no" to them. You just couldn't say "no."

It was a pity Phil wasn't here. Get him on an anti-vytoc rant or a reminiscence about Chicago and nobody would be able to get another word in for the rest of the evening. Fortunately, she did have someone handy who was almost as good at monopolizing a conversation.

"I hear you got the part of Lynessa," Carlina said to her sister.

"Yeah, can't believe it. And Pete Messel gets to be Vyn! The freechen penthouse! If he kisses me, I'll faint – really! Professor Wylkensen's gonna direct and I hope Mrs. Gregor does the costumes this time. She's the one who did the dresses for *Babes in the Badlands...*"

And so it went for the rest of the meal.

Once the leftovers were sequestered into their proper

containers, and the sauce removed from the children, Carlina was able to put the spaghetti out of her mind for a little while; along with all thoughts of her otherworldly benefactor.

Until, of course, the speech came on, and she had to look at him, standing quietly at the Prefect's right elbow.

Viewing the speech wasn't exactly mandatory, but there was nothing else on and, besides, it was guaranteed to be a main topic of conversation for the next few days no matter where you went.

"They moved *Moons of Tillyn* for this?" Christina groaned. "It's the same thing he said in his State of the City speech."

"Perhaps it's all they could muster at the last minute," suggested Nigel. "You didn't hear if something happened to his speechwriter?"

"Nah, just him. Two shots in the head. That's why he's wearing that funny hat. Though I don't see why he has to make a whole speech, anyway. Why can't he just come out and say, 'Hi, guys; I'm all right,' and go away?"

"He's a politician, isn't he?" Nigel countered. "You know if their lot speak for less than half an hour, their tongues seize up."

"That's a bad thing?"

"Well, now that you mention it..."

"Wonder if it hurts," Christina said, changing subjects in midstream. "Having that crystal stuck in your neck. Or perhaps they don't feel pain. The Prefect don't seem too bothered about gettin' shot."

"I think it does hurt for a while," Carlina answered her. "But it goes away quickly. Cass said she was told it's a little like a baby cutting a tooth."

"More like gettin' bit if you ask me. Don't know why she wanted to do it."

"Immortality mostly," Carlina sighed. *And her relationship with Mr. Géricault,* she added to herself.

She looked up at the man on the screen. He was like most vytoc: tall and pale, with dark hair and crystal-blue eyes. Handsome, rich, and powerful. What girl could resist?

But what do you want with me? She asked silently of the man on the screen. *What could I possibly give you?*

Chapter Three

The Prefect returned to his normal duties the next day and, without a state funeral to keep their interest up, the news services turned their attention to other things as well: like a string of produce robberies and the continuing controversy regarding contaminated water at a new hydro. There was also another scandal in the works involving Saylor Doering, the City's notorious political boss. Some had noticed that the most recent Council elections had been followed immediately by sudden increases in the price of painkillers and other common medicines – but only in those districts which had rejected candidates backed by Doering. Naturally, any accusations of price gouging had been repudiated, with the most forceful denials coming from Aesculapian Pharmaceuticals, where Doering was CFO.

Two weeks later and the attack on the Prefect had largely been forgotten. Life in Titan City went on as it always had...

And Phil was venturing outside the dome.

Although his first attempt had nearly killed him, Phil had since learned of safer means to leave the city. Now a citizen, he could ride along with the pharmaceutical vans bringing drugs and medical equipment to the hospital in Tylerville. This had meant getting up at a horrible hour -- and on a Monday, no less! But it got him away from Titan City for at least one morning a week. He was usually back by lunchtime.

Phil liked Tylerville. The people were friendly and vytoc nonexistent. Better yet, the price of food was lower, as Tylerville acted as the main processor for the agro-colonies. He usually brought back a little something for Nigel and Carlina.

The "Old Colony" (as Tylerville was still called officially) lay some twenty miles or so to the north of Titan City; connected by a single, six-lane, divided highway. Known simply as the "Commercial Route," this was a very straight and to-the-point road; the realm of truckers and other people who care more for efficient drive time than pretty scenery. The picturesque rivers and hills along the way were purely incidental.

But there was a junction...

Marked only with a warning to watch for merging traffic, the unnamed tributary forked off from the Commercial Route about two miles from Titan's industrial ring. It stretched out an unknown distance to the southwest, despite there being no sign of human habitation in that direction.

Phil had always wondered where it led. He was still wondering.

"Sorry, pal. She's a dead end."

Laas Carolsyn shifted the van into reverse as Phil gazed forlornly at the gate blocking the roadway. Though he knew Laas would not be able to take the entire route, he had hoped they could go a little farther than this.

"Think there's a way to bypass the circuit?"

"If you're a vytoc," Laas answered. "And I wouldn't put it past them to have it armed in some way. Facilitators are very good at letting you know when they don't want you nosing about."

"I wonder if my motorcycle..."

"You're on your own there, buddy. And you'd better have on a good exosuit and plenty of oxygen, not to mention extra fuel. I've heard it goes for more than a hundred miles."

"But to where?" Phil wondered aloud.

"The spaceport."

"The wha?!" He was suddenly sitting very straight.

Laas laughed.

"It's just a joke, really," he explained. "All the old ships the Facilitators took from Earth are out there. You can see them from the Mayor's Tower when the wind's not kickin' up the dust. Back when I was a kid, they had a news crew sneak out there; made a big production about it. But they didn't find anything beyond a lot of wreckage."

"At least that's what they said, anyway."

"Could be something out there, could be nothing," Laas shrugged. "Or, it could be something the tockers have since dismantled. The only thing you can bet on is that if there's a real spaceport hidden away in all that junk, it'll be guarded by the Devils themselves. And you won't be getting past them. You don't go playing games with vytoc, Phil. If they want you to stay here, you'll stay."

"I don't agree with that."

"I know. Still true, though."

Laas merged the van back onto the Commercial Route while Phil stretched out on the bench seat behind the driver's saddle. Before them loomed the massive dome and towers of the city.

Phil had long been an avid reader of science fiction, and one of his biggest beefs with Titan City was that it didn't look the way he thought it should.

In his mind, if people were going to go to the trouble of constructing a giant dome around a city, then the city should should damn well *fit inside* the dome, much in the same way a ship built in a bottle stays entirely in the bottle. At least that was how they built domed cities in *Astounding*, or *Amazing Stories*.

But whoever built Titan must not have read those magazines. Here, the towers jutted out on all sides, like a Cubist porcupine. In the centre, the tallest towers reached nearly a hundred stories above the dome, as though they were trees growing through the greenhouse roof. The overall effect not only mixed metaphors, it was just...cluttered.

In comparison, Tylerville consisted of eighteen dome-shaped buildings arranged in three circles; connected by tunnel-like roadways. It might be barely half the size of Chicago's Loop, and could support only a tiny fraction of Titan's population, but at least it *looked* like a space colony.

"Y'know, Phil. I've always wondered something."

"Like what?"

"Like why you come back." Laas gave him a brief look. "I mean, I know you've got restrictions when you're a Newcomer. But you're a Citizen now. Why don't you just stay in Tylerville?"

"Probably will, one of these days," Phil said. "But right now, I've got work to do. Been helping a friend out. You know."

"The one with the motorcycle?"

"Yeah. But once that's out of the way? Definitely! Dr. Vasser even said he'd find me a position in the children's clinic. 'Course, I'd rather find the spaceport."

"You'll have better luck in Tylerville."

"They got a spaceport?"

"Well, it's where they film *Moons of Tillyn.* That's about as good as you're going to get, I'm afraid."

"Knowing my luck, I'll end up on the set of *Tower Eighteen* instead."

That brought another laugh from Laas. *Tower Eighteen* was a resistance drama.

"Better look alive then, Mr. Davis," Laas joked, referring to *Tower Eighteen's* rebel hero. "We're at the gate."

Phil sat up again as the van approached the gigantic airlock that was Titan City's main entrance. The gateway extended out from the dome, so that up to eight vans could fit between the hatches at any given time.

This morning, they were lucky in that only two other vans shared the gateway with them. That meant the customs inspection should be over with quicker than usual.

A green light went on, letting everyone know the air was breathable and the drivers began getting out of their vans. While Phil stretched his legs, Laas opened the cargo bay doors and the customs team emerged from their offices on the city side. Phil noted with some irritation that two of the inspectors were wearing the jade green uniforms of the Security Services.

"Hi'ya, Frank!" Laas called out as the chief inspector came their way. "Catch any more of those hot springs flatworms?"

"Why? You feelin' hungry?"

"Well, it's lunchtime by my clock!"

Phil had never seen, let alone eaten, a hot springs flatworm, but a local urban legend told of Titanian restaurants serving up the creatures as "Terran Eel." Rumours of customs agents accepting bribes to allow flatworms into the city were rife among Titan's truck drivers. Laas liked to joke that the bribe in question was a lightly grilled flatworm with capers and lemon sauce.

Titan's answer to rats in the fried chicken, Phil mused as he watched Laas sign the customs ticket and the Security men inspected their cargo.

"Got anything out of the ordinary," the chief inspector was saying. "Or been given anything unusual or suspicious or otherwise outside of your normal guidelines?"

"Got a box of motorcycle parts," Laas answered. "Belongs to the guy over there."

"You have a motorcycle, sir?"

"Yessir," Phil told the inspector. "A Vorhees 165. Got the new overhaul kit."

"You'll let us take a look at it."

It wasn't a question. And a moot point at best, since the Security men had already opened the case and were going through the parts. After a cursory examination, they slid the case back into the van and closed the cargo bay doors.

"They're clean."

Laas took his receipt and motioned for Phil to get back in the van. A little while later, the gateway's inner hatches opened up and they drove on into the City.

The Commercial Route came to an end among the warehouses of level 10, a section of the city comparable to Chicago's Back-of-the-Yards. Understandably, Laas chose not to stick around, heading immediately for the interior freeway known as the Periphery. This wide ramp curved along the perimeter of the dome from level 10, all the way up to 110. In Titan's claustrophobic network of flats and rampways, the

Periphery was the only means for a large vehicle to get anywhere with ease.

At about level 50, Laas took the van inward and Phil tightened his seatbelt.

Like Nigel and the computers, Phil had yet to get comfortable with Titanian vehicles. They were triangular in shape: the driver sitting alone in front, with the passengers confined to the bench seat behind him. It might be an odd-looking arrangement, but it did give the driver an uninterrupted view on both sides, something you needed when navigating the glorified game of 'Snakes and Ladders' that was Titan City. Add traffic and pedestrians and...well, Phil was forever amazed that there weren't more accidents. He shuddered to think about what would happen should Laas miss a turn.

"All right, Phil. You can open your eyes now."

Dr. Nielsen looked up just as the van coasted through the level 70 service tunnel of Tower 9. They pulled up beside a pair of vans bearing the logo of Aesculapian Pharmaceuticals.

"End of the line, pal. Same time next week?"

"Wouldn't miss it for the world."

The motorcycle parts had not been put back very neatly, and it took a few moments of rearranging before Phil could get the case latched again. With a little help from Laas, he was soon heading for the elevators, his case in one hand and a bag of groceries in the other.

Checking his watch, he determined that it was only just now noon. Everybody in the lab would be out to lunch -- with the notable exception of Dr. Lionel Swendon, one of their junior researchers.

As it turned out, there were actually four people left in the laboratory. Phil found Swendon with three interns, playing a video game someone had called up on the lab's main communicator screen. He gave the little group a casual wave as he set the grocery bag down at Nigel's work station.

"Don't suppose any of you know where Nage ran off to?"

"They're over at Minta's," Lionel said, not taking his eyes from the screen. "The 'B' room, I think."

"Thanks. See ya later."

As he left the lab, Phil overheard a comment from one of the interns.

"Minta's? I thought they all went to the Underpass."

But he didn't bother about waiting to hear Lionel's answer. It would have been a lie anyway.

In an unexpected stroke of good timing, he got to the elevators just as a car opened up and within minutes, he was strolling through the wide lobby and out onto the flat.

Minta's Sandwich Shop and Catering Service was located across the flat from the hospital's entrance. It was your basic grab-and-go eatery, with most of the customers either taking lunch back to the office or eating at one of the many little tables set outside. As he stood in line, Phil idly watched the people milling about.

There were only two or three who could have passed for white.

Eight years and it still felt odd being one of the racial majority. Even stranger was the fact that he was the only one who seemed to notice – or care! In all this time, he had yet to hear anyone utter a racial epithet of any kind. The exception, of course, was "tocker," but you wouldn't call a fellow human that.

It was a different story back home. Race matters in Chicago and in that regard, Phil had been permanently marked by his mother.

Not that it was her fault. His parents, both immigrants, had met in an English class for new citizens, where a common knowledge of French helped to bring them together. They even timed their marriage to coincide with their naturalization, and Phil was born about seven months later. Unfortunately, though, while his father was an X-ray technician with a good-paying job, the family had been unable to buy a house or live anywhere better than a miserable two-flat on the city's southwest side. The reason being that nobody would sell a proper house to a family that was mostly black.

School had been a nightmare. The Navy, slightly better, but still no picnic, since America's armed forces hadn't been integrated very long when he'd joined. He fared a little better in England, mainly because he was an American and therefore seen as somewhat exotic. Medical school wasn't too bad, though he was one of only six blacks in his class. Despite the obstacles, he'd managed to earn plenty of recognition in his academic endeavours. In the end, however, all the honours in the world couldn't help him to land a job. His position at Swedish American was largely the result of his father calling in a favour.

So many frustrations, so many roadblocks in his way, and why? Because his skin was a darker colour than his father's.

But he was still his father's son, dammit! And therefore just as Swedish as Lara *and* Lara's worthless brother!

He thought back bitterly to the moment at their wedding, when the pastor had asked if anyone knew of a reason why the couple shouldn't be joined in holy matrimony. Lara's brother had stood up and announced to the entire congregation that Lara shouldn't marry Phil because Phil was a black man.

Except he didn't say "black man." He'd used a different word.

And yet, Phil yearned to return home, for Lara's sake if nothing else. Really, if Mr. Port had been more forthcoming (and had allowed him to bring his wife along) he would have happily volunteered to live here. It was the whole abduction thing that did it. The fact that Facilitators didn't appreciate the difference between recruiting and kidnapping was what kept him forever searching for a way out.

"Hey, Moon Trooper! You plannin' to order?"

"What? Oh, sorry," Phil said, his mind returning to the sandwich counter. "I'd like the chicken on wheat with the pepper sauce. Cheesy nibs on the side."

"Anything to drink?"

"Yeah. A small CytriSuds, please."

"That'll be 23 sestri."*

Phil connected his bank card to the reader. The number on the card's tiny readout screen reduced itself by 23, signifying that the transaction was complete.

That was another thing about Titan City: no paper money. And you rarely saw anybody using pocket change for amounts over 10 sestri. But Phil was forced to admit that this was another of Titan's good points. Bank cards were insured and couldn't be used if you declared them stolen. There were still muggers and pickpockets in Titan City, but they were usually more interested in getting ration books than actual cash.

Phil picked up his food, stashing his sandwich in his work satchel as he still carried the case of motorcycle parts. Casually, he walked to the back of the shop, where the meeting rooms were kept.

There was a young man loitering in the hall next to

---

* A sestrus is equivalent to a dollar in American money. Wheat bread sandwiches are expensive in Titan City.

meeting room B, seemingly preoccupied with playing a hand-held game. As Dr. Nielsen approached, he looked up and quietly pushed open the door.

"At last! The man we've been waiting for!"

A short, portly man stood up to greet him as Phil slid his case onto the meeting table. Already on the table was an identical case, filled with a similar assortment of parts. *That* had been last week's little errand.

"Had a run-in with the SS on the way in," he told the man in charge. "But I think everything's still there."

"Excellent! You've done a fine job, Doctor."

Now free of his burden, Phil found an empty chair and began eating his lunch. The other men around the table were a motley mix of middle-aged executive types in business suits and college kids with their shirt sleeves cut into strips – the latest fashion trend for upper level youth.

Moving down from the head of the table was the excessively stout form of Saylor Doering. Thanks to the high price of food, any Titanian who was fat and could not give evidence of a glandular condition was thought to be either very rich or very corrupt. In Doering's case, he was both, though still a paean of virtue when compared with the typical Chicago alderman.

"Mr. Vyncent!" He was saying to one of the college boys. "I believe you know how these fit together?"

"Of course, Mr. Doering."

The young man stood up and began to sort through the parts, taking some apart and reattaching others. In minutes, his assemblage had assumed the unmistakable shape of a small bore rifle.

Phil raised an eyebrow.

"*That's* the new super-weapon?" He asked, incredulously.

"Don't let its look deceive you," answered Doering. "Granted, it's still incomplete and the bullets are a long way from ready, but yes, this is the gun."

He took the weapon from Mr. Vyncent and held it up to the light.

"Gentleman, you see before you the next phase of human resistance. The first gun ever made that can bring down a vytoc with one shot. And, what's more!" He gave them all a toothy grin. "He won't be getting up again."

There was a burst of cheering, and back-slapping from the other men. Phil, however, remained sceptical. The gun looked far too small to be a threat to anything larger than a squirrel.

"I'll believe it when I see it."

"Oh, you will," Mr. Doering assured him. "Things are afoot, you see. Bit by bit we are chipping away at their leadership; destroying their confidence in their own kind. Last month's little incident is still rattling nerves in the Liaison Office, and I assure you, that was only the beginning! Since then, I've put a few other little pieces into play. Soon, they'll be wondering just how far our network extends."

Phil tried not to choke.

"Like I told you when the assassination when down," he said. "The Cat already knows the network's in the hospital. I don't see what you're gonna do to change his mind on that."

"No, you wouldn't, would you?" Doering gave him a patronizing smile. "But we're never going to get anywhere unless we can redirect a little of the heat. Unfortunately, Facilitators are beyond bribery, being as they have little need for either food or money. So, we'll give them a different kind of present: a little taste of victory before the battle really begins!"

This time Phil kept quiet as Doering received another round of applause; remaining firmly unconvinced that the Facilitators would fall for the ruse, whatever it was. The Cat had already shown himself to be a shrewd sonofabitch. It would take more than a simple red herring to pull the wool over *his* eyes.

Honestly, he wondered sometimes why he kept up with this bunch of amateurs. Surely, the Security Services would have them all arrested in a heartbeat if there were even the slightest chance that they posed an actual threat. About the only thing he could say in his defence was that at least it was something. Even a dunderheaded resistance was better than none at all.

He finished his sandwich and made his good-bye's:

"Sorry, can't stick around. Got work waitin' for me."

Saylor Doering caught his arm.

"I've found a place on the East Curve." he said in Phil's ear. "Tower 30, level 48. Used to be an old foreman's club back during the construction. I trust you're still willing to help with the training?"

"Sure. What time you want me?"

"Saturday. 18 hours."

"Right. I'll be there."

"Thank you, Doctor."

"Anytime, Mr. Doering."

Chapter Four

The Cat was feeling rather put out.

Despite persistent rumours to the contrary, he didn't know *everything* that went on in the city. Really, who'd want to? But today it would've been nice to have had a little of that fabled omniscience. He knew he was being kept from something and the very thought rankled.

"Yer bein' awful quiet there, mate."

"Don't feel like talking."

Kittyvoc* gazed absent-mindedly out the Land Rover's window as Fosteperon guided the SUV up the ramp and into the parking area of Titan's University of Applied Science.

Facilitators generally drove Earth-made vehicles and the Security Services in particular kept two Land Rovers on reserve. This one was right-side steering and Fosteperon considered it "his," even going so far as to personalize it with a small, plush kola bear that hung from the rear-view mirror. A bit cutesy perhaps for a police vehicle, but Kittyvoc decided not to fight it. There were always more important things to worry about. The current mission, for a start.

"I understand they had to twist yer arm a bit for this one."

"Strung up by the thumbs is more like it."

"Think there's something here, then?"

---

* Pronounced kit'-eh-vok. The name, as one might expect, inspired the nickname, although "Cat" was a compromise of sorts. The alternative was to have everyone calling him "Kitty."

"Almost certainly. That's the problem."

Special Investigator Alrund had drawn up the profiles and there had been some very specific information given as to what they should look for. It struck Kittyvoc as being a little *too* specific. In particular, the list of names. Or rather, the *name*. It was all too detailed; too exact. And none of it rang true. Especially the girl. There was no reason for the girl.

"Wake up, boss. We're here."

Fosteperon pulled the Land Rover into a space marked RESERVED FOR VISITORS, waiting a few minutes for the underpowered Titanian police vans to catch up with them before getting out.

"Ready?"

"Might as well get it over with."

"Right. I'll get the boys kitted up."

"Stun wands only, Foz. We're dealing with kids here."

"What about you then?" Fosteperon gave a nod toward Kittyvoc's holster.

"Just an accessory."

"Got hat an' shoes to go with it, then?"

"I've got a boot."

"Fair enough. I'll be gettin' the wands."

Facilitators seldom used weapons of any sort. They didn't need to. The human agents working as support staff, however, received stun wands, though they could be given small calibre handguns should the need warrant it. Kittyvoc's holster, meanwhile, contained a Mauser C96 "broom handle" pistol -- but it was purely for show.

You couldn't get much uglier or more intimidating than a Mauser C96. It was primitive and clunky, and looked very much like what you would get if a rifle maker tried to design a handgun. It even fired rifle rounds, and the polished wooden holster could double as a shoulder stock.

And it would jam after every shot, which was why Kittyvoc generally kept it unloaded. But he did carry a few blanks in his pocket, just in case.

As Fosteperon handed out the stun wands, a few students walked past, eyes widening at the sight of the Cat. *Better make this quick,* he thought to himself, *the wider the eyes, the bigger the mouths.*

"All right, men," he addressed the agents. "The suspect is said to be a pale-skinned full-Caucasian with light brown hair – and I want you to forget right now that anybody ever told you that. Suspect everyone and assume nothing, am I understood? Good. Peters, take this entrance. Kosk and Lewys, you'll work the entrance at 75. You see anyone, tell 'em to go back to their rooms. Nobody's leaving 'till we say so.

"The rest of you, follow me."

As they set off, Agent Peters gave his comrades a happy little wave of farewell, knowing he had been given the cushy post.

Level 70 wasn't a proper flat, just a pair of rampways leading into the parking garage. The real entrance to the

University was on level 75, where most of the students came and went. In between, however, were the student living areas, the places where the Security men were likely to run into, if not a lot of trouble, than at least a lot of lip.

"Can I help you gentlemen?"

The "Arad," or Residential Administrator, was standing squarely in the middle of the main hallway. She was putting on a very brave front, considering she was one small human being facing down a pair of vytoc backed by a full security team.

"We've had word of some weapons being stored here," Kittyvoc told her. "We'll only be a minute."

"Oh ... well," she said, perplexed. "You'll need to register...and get your visitor passes."

"I have a pass already." He showed her his badge, holding it directly against the crystal at his throat so that the metal sparked along the edge.

"Uh, yeah....So I guess you can...go."

"Thank you."

"Nice stall there, y'think?" commented Fosteperon, as they made their way to the verticals.

"From an episode of *Tower Eighteen*. Though I believe the Facilitators actually took the time to register in that one."

"Not playing by the script, are we?"

"Of course we are. Ours is just the rewritten version. I'd say now's a good time to run the com check."

As they reached the elevators, Fosteperon slid his communication headset up onto his head. Behind them, the seven remaining agents did the same. After a few minutes of babble ("...com check 1,1...come in...com check 1,2...say again, Kosk...com check 1,3...") everything was declared to be in working order. Agents Kosk and Lewys were allowed into the vertical and Kittyvoc waited until the car had reached level 75 before shutting down the system.

"Now them," he said to the remaining men. "This level is largely cafeterias and common rooms. Jensen, you're good with kids, look around and see if you can get anyone to talk with you. And don't discount the sarcasm. Let them get carried away with their insults, and they'll often tell you things they didn't intend to. As for the rest of you, we'll be concentrating on the men's dormitory. Hopefully we won't have to do it, but we know they've had warning, so we might have to continue on to the women's levels as well. Keep on the lookout for anyone sitting suspiciously or who otherwise looks as though he might be hiding something. If you meet anyone armed, don't engage them. Leave the fighting to Mr. Foster and myself. Understood?"

With a chorus of "Understood," the agents split off. Jensen headed for the common rooms while the others divided themselves among the stairwells. They would be working levels 73 and 74 as well as the stairs. You always found somebody sitting on the stairs.

"You! Open your satchels for inspection!"

"But...it's just books, sir."

"Then the inspection will be a quick one. Go on – open them...right. You're good. Carry on."

And on into the dormitory proper.

"Open up! Room inspection!"

"We're not doin' nuthin'!"

"Doesn't matter. Security Services – open up!"

And so it went, the Cat spreading his usual good will throughout the dormitories. Fortunately, the students were being cooperative today and not giving him the usual sass, at least not to his face. He did catch a few comments once his back was turned but he let them go.

To tell the truth, he didn't particularly like working student areas. Normally, the Security Services left kids alone, leaving any disturbances to the regular police. Nor was he particularly alarmed by the possibility of resistance activity here. In his opinion, young people *should* resist. What else was youth for?

But the Liaison Office had been in an awful state ever since the assassination. For while the Prefect might be fine, the same could not be said for the car he was riding in. Portysanon had been absolutely livid when he saw the damage to his beloved Cadillac. Obviously, someone was going to pay -- for the window, at any rate.

Kittyvoc had nearly covered his half of the 74th floor

when his communicator crackled to life.

"Cat. It's Foz. We've got a possible on 73. Requesting backup."

"On my way!"

Using his linking crystal, Kittyvoc pinpointed Fosteperon's exact location on the floor below. Then he took the stairwell that would put him at the opposite end of the hall. But the caution proved unnecessary. He found his lieutenant leaning casually against a closed dorm-room door.

"Has a mechanical lock on it. Figured I'd give you the honours."

"What are friends for?"

Unholstering the Mauser, Kittyvoc gave the door a swift kick, his jackboot splitting the thin wood with ease. Pulling out what remained of the door with his free hand, he walked in to find two young men pointing pistols at him.

They didn't seem too keen on firing, though. Obviously, they knew just enough about firearms to note the size of the Mauser's ammunition chamber.

"Second thoughts, boys?"

Wordlessly, the guns came down. Fosteperon stepped past Kittyvoc and pulled the weapons from their hands.

But were those the only guns?

Kittyvoc scanned the room. It was a typical engineering-school dorm, liberally cluttered with books, computer components, food wrappers, dirty laundry, kinetic sculptures, and for some reason, a scale model of tower 16 done in ice cream spoons. In the far corner sat a latched laundry hamper.

Such hampers were popular going-off-to-college gifts and this one was richly decorated with meschelwood panels and brass trim. It had a set of wheels and a telescoping handle for easy transport to the laundry facility. Most students had something like it. Occasionally, they even put laundry in them.

"Let's take a look in there, shall we?"

"Why there?"

"Yeah! It's obvious he never uses it," cracked the second young man.

"My thoughts exactly. Now, open it."

Giving his friend a vicious look, the room's primary occupant nudged the laundry bin open with his foot. Revealed was a wadded mass of mildewed gym towels, and a stench that took up a space all its own.

"There. See." He began to close the lid again.

"Not so fast there, Stinky," Fosteperon said, upending the bin completely. The towels fell out, followed by two large metal cases.

"I'd say you should wash those by hand."

"I don't know how they got there. Honest!"

"Don't you, now." Kittyvoc picked up the two cases and opened up the lighter one. Inside were six padded compartments, four of which held Vyn type 12 pistols -- the same kind of pistols the boys had been holding.

"I suppose you found those other two Vyns just lying on the bed?"

"Yeah!"

"Reckon the pistol fairy brings 'em." Fosteperon grinned.

"I don't know how they got there, all right!"

"Right. Your name, son."

"Silas Doering."

"And your relationship to Saylor Doering?"

"He's my da — UNCLE!"

"Your d'uncle is he? And how about you?" Kittyvoc turned to the other young man.

"Laurence Wittyn. No relation."

"Really," Kittyvoc deadpanned, sifting through the half-truths. Terryl Wittyn was a prominent member of the Civic Council and it was no secret that he had a son at the University. And, while it may not have been in the official paperwork, it was common knowledge that Councilman Wittyn's closest campaign advisor was none other than Saylor Doering. Hardly a coincidence then, that the children of these two men would be friends as well.

By now, the other agents had figured out that the search was over and were gathering in the hall outside the broken threshold. Fosteperon traded the gun cases for a stun wand, which he proceeded to point at the two boys.

"Time to go! With me, now. Come on – both of you!"

"Why me? It's his room!"

"Sorry Mister Not-That-Laurence-Wittyn. Both of you were pointing guns. Both of you are under arrest. Now, get along!"

Reluctantly, the two men slunk out the door, followed by Fosteperon. Kittyvoc held back just long enough to radio the all clear.

"Fall back to the vans, men. Mission complete."

"Uh, Cat? This is Jensen. Mission not quite complete, sir."

"What is it, Jensen?"

"It's Lewys, sir."

"Lewys is guarding the upper entrances."

"Er...actually, he's down here with me."

"What in Hell is he doing down there?"

"Ah...er...he thought he could do more here...um, he was, well he was looking for someone and I think he found her. We're...we're having some issues in the cafeteria. I...uh...I think we could use some backup."

Kittyvoc snarled a few choice invectives in his native Serbian, causing several doors down the hall to suddenly slam shut. The students listening in may not have understood the language, but they heard the emotion behind it loud and clear. Whoever Lewys was, he was big trouble.

"Foz, get the primaries to base," Kittyvoc snapped into the com. "I'll aid Jensen."

"Right, Cat. We're off!"

Taking a moment to load a blank into the Mauser, Kittyvoc headed back down to the common areas. He found Jensen sombrely waiting for him outside the cafeteria. Through the door came the sound of muffled chanting.

"You really don't want to go in there," the agent said as Kittyvoc walked up.

"What happened?"

Jensen took a deep breath, clearly unhappy about being made the stool pigeon.

"Ah. Well, sir...I was working the game rooms – played a bit of table tennis, some electrosoccer – and I think I was making progress, but...well, Mack came down saying he had to find somebody down here – some girl."

"And?"

Kittyvoc kept his voice steady, but something was beginning to fall into place here and he didn't like what it was forming. Meanwhile, the hapless Jensen stared forlornly at his boots.

"Well, sir...er. Mack's not very good with kids, you know. He lacks a bit of...well..."

"Sympathy?"

"Yessir! Sympathy."

"Right," Kittyvoc sighed. "Who'd he pick a fight with

this time?"

"I wouldn't call it a fight, sir. More like a scuffle. But he did slap the girl about a few times. Mind you, I'd say she was asking for it."

"So, he's beating up little girls..."

"You shouldn't put it like that sir."

"Ask a ghost child. This happened in the cafeteria?"

"No, sir. The reading room. That's where he found her. But she made a run for it and we...well..."

The agent fell silent.

"Take your time," Kittyvoc said, irritably. "I am immortal, after all."

"She went into the cafeteria," Jensen continued softly. "I think they were waiting for him. I'm not getting into any trouble for this, am I?"

"You? No. Get back to the van." Kittyvoc dismissed the agent and opened the doors to the cafeteria...

...And walked into a minor riot.

"GREEN BEAN! GREEN BEAN!

STANDING ALL ALONE!

GREEN BEAN! GREEN BEAN!

WHY DON'T YOU GO HOME!"

Agent Lewis was standing hunched in the middle of a large group of students, blindly waving his stun wand; hitting nothing. Meanwhile, the students were dancing in a circle, chanting nursery rhymes, and pelting him with what looked like the contents of the garbage chute.

"GREEN BEAN! GREEN BEAN!

KNOCK 'EM ON THE FLOOR!

GIVE OL' BEAN A SWIFT SWEEP

AND SEND HIM OUT THE DOOR!"

There was no use in shouting. Kittyvoc pointed the Mauser up at the ceiling and fired. As the shot echoed off the walls, the students froze. All eyes turned to look at the Cat.

Agent Lewys straightened up, brushed the garbage from his shoulders, and grabbed the arm of a woman standing nearby.

"It's her, sir," he said, firmly. "She started it."

"Really," Kittyvoc said, unimpressed. "And what is your name, young lady?"

"Christina Manning. Cassandra's sister."

It was, unfortunately, the answer he had been expecting. That was the name on the profile, though he hadn't ordered anyone to actually look for the girl. So, why was Lewys so intent on arresting her? Then again, why did Alrund want her arrested in the first place.

"You set up the ambush?"

"Could have."

"Well, then, you're coming with us."

"You can't do that! He started it! Him and his big mouth, comin' in here like he owns the place!"

"You little..." Lewys raised a hand.

"Hit her and I'll break your neck," Kittyvoc growled, noting the looks of triumph in the faces around them. There was another story here and he didn't need an upstart human getting in the way.

"But really, I can't go." The girl pleaded. "It's Wednesday! I gotta look after my sister's kids!"

"Should have thought about that before you started throwing things, shouldn't you."

"I'm not a member of the Resistance, honest!"

"This isn't an arrest," Kittyvoc assured her, his voice softening. "You're just going into protective custody."

"Protective from what?"

"Well, we wouldn't want what happened to your sister to happen to you, now do we?"

"What? You mean find a husband, get married, and have a couple kids?"

Yes, very clever, thought Kittyvoc. But while he wasn't exactly in the mood, he was willing to play along with this one.

"A horrible fate," he told her, sounding as pompous as he could. "That we certainly wouldn't want to befall a talented young woman like yourself. So, to counteract any event that could result in the condition known as 'motherhood,' we shall thus remove you from the perilous influences of young men."

"What!"

Snickers could be heard among the surrounding students.

"Oh, you are a bastard!"

"I do have a reputation to maintain. Take her out of here, Lewys."

Marching with an impressive goose-step, the girl left with Lewys in her train. Kittyvoc looked around at the remaining mess and slowly shook his head.

"You gonna arrest us as well?" Asked a voice in the crowd.

"Kid. When the Arad sees this, you'll wish we had."

Chapter Five

"Look, Carlina. I'm sorry, but she's here under special authority of the Security Services. I'm not able to just go in and let her go."

"I thought you had friends in the Security Services."

"I do, for the most part. But this is an official matter."

Mr. Géricault was doing his level best to look small and ineffectual, aided in part by the limited frame of Carlina's desktop communicator.

"It's no good to step on toes, you know."

"You will at least speak with them?" Carlina said in earnest, not yet ready to resign herself to taking the afternoon off.

The Facilitator rubbed at his chin for a moment, as though a thought were just now occurring to him.

"I suppose it's possible that something might be worked out. But it would involve some concessions on your part."

"What sort of concessions?"

"Well, you know, of course, that before Cassandra died, she made certain arraignments with us. And with her death, those promises were left unfulfilled."

Carlina stared at the communicator in shock. Surely, he wasn't suggesting that she carry out what Cassandra had planned?

"That was between you and Cass," she replied, regaining her composure. "I can't really see what it has to do with me."

"My dear Carlina," cajoled the Facilitator. "Your sister was about to embark on a historic journey! To become the first person born on Latebra to make the transition from human to vytoc. And, since the system has already been formatted for her genetic print, it is only logical that a close relative should be the one to take her place."

"I can't do that!" Carlina cried. "I'm married ... have children! I can't just leave them for...for..."

"For immortality? The glory of Titan City? Betterment of the human race? ...Your sister's memory?"

Mr. Géricault gazed out at her, almost pleadingly.

"Then I'm afraid there's nothing I can do," he said, coldly. "Sorry, Carlina. I'll make sure you are the first to know if Christina is released."

The communicator went dark.

Carlina angrily knocked the screen aside, resting her head in her hands. The sides of her face burned wet as she lost the battle against her tears.

As if having Chris arrested wasn't bad enough! But to have him bring up Cassi like that? Maybe it was for the best that she was leaving early today.

"You all right, Dr. White?"

Carlina turned to find a small girl hanging from her

office door. The child was holding onto the knobs and swinging, so that the door pulled her slowly back and forth across the floor.

"Yes, Serena, I'm fine. Just angry is all." She found a handkerchief and wiped her eyes. "Sometimes it's easy to forget they don't think the way we do."

"Not really. They think like people," said Serena, sagely. "It's just that things don't happen to them the way they do us. They don't gots the same consequences."

"Don't learn their lessons. Is that it?"

"Yeah!"

Serena was only nine, looked six, and talked like thirty. The latter, no doubt, a result of having been around scientists her whole life. That she was hanging around here and not in school was a consequence of her being a ghost child; the albino offspring of a vytasynene addict.

Such children were a result of bioengineering gone awry. What was now Titan City's most notorious drug had been originally developed to fight rejection in organ transplants. But the drug's ability to realign cells was overshadowed by it's effects on brain chemistry: it was an absolutely perfect truth serum.

Unfortunately, any practical usage was mitigated by the fact that anyone not immediately killed by the drug was permanently addicted to it. And withdrawal was ever bit as deadly as an overdose.

Worst of all, was the effect it had on children born to addicted mothers. The drug not only addicted them in the womb, it altered their genetic structure. Most notably, they lacked any sort of pigmentation. In Titan's dark-skinned society, they were easily noticed, and just as easily outcast.

As for Serena, Carlina had known her mother ever since primary school. She and Gaila had interned together in the same laboratory, working for three years on a project to find a cure for the addiction. Prevented, understandably, from using human subjects, Gaila had gone so far as to inject herself with the drug in an attempt to get a first-hand account of its effects.

In that, she had gotten far more than she'd bargained for. Twelve years later, they still hadn't found a way for an addict to safely withdraw from vytasynene. And so Gaila had ended up passing her addiction on to another generation.

And while Titanians might be blind to issues of race, they had little tolerance for ghost children. Serena and her brother were banned from attending city schools and it would be a miracle if either of them could get a proper job once they grew up. Gaila tried her best to give them an education, finding tutors where she could. Most of these were her friends and fellow medical professionals; so the children had acquired a near-encyclopedic knowledge of anatomy and biochemistry. Serena in particular, had proved herself a handy assistant in the pharmacy. It was a pity the girl could have no future there.

"Muncie says, if you want to get anything out of a vytoc, you have'ta send the Devil after 'em," she was saying, still swinging on the door.

"Why the Devil?"

"'Cause the Devil understands consequences!"

And ghost children cannot lie, Carlina thought to herself. And neither were they capable of speaking metaphorically. Was there a literal devil that could rescue Christina?

The question continued to gnaw at her as she joined Nigel and the others for lunch. There was one more than usual today as Dr. Peris had decided to join in. Nevertheless, Carlina was so lost in thought that she walked right past all three of them standing quite clearly in the centre of the lobby.

"Something on your mind 'Lina?"

"It's Chris."

Briefly, she told them about her sister's arrest and the complete lack of help she had received from Mr. Géricault. She declined, however, to tell them about his "offer."

"You did explain that once they're in college it's too late for a virgin sacrifice?"

"Phil!"

"Listen, seriously," Dr. Nielsen said, backing away as Carlina swung her work satchel at him. "Sometimes they just pinch people to make a statement. There've been guys in the Resistance who've been put in one of those infirmary rooms

like they had us in. Never questioned-- then released for
no good reason."

"You do hear rumours, though," said Dr. Peris,
sounding concerned.

"Yeah. You get stories," Phil countered. "Usually from
people who like to tell stories. Come to think of it, that may be
the real reason why they took her."

"Because she has a big mouth?"

"Because she's got a big imagination. It's no secret
she's a theatre rat."

"The anti-ghost child," Nigel commented. "And
forgive me for changing the subject, but where does everyone
want to eat? I'm famished!"

"The Underpass?" Dr. Peris offered.

"I'm game," seconded Phil, and the Doctors White
quickly agreed.

The Underpass Café and Cider Press was one of the
more popular restaurants in the middle levels as it was located
near enough to the dome wall to allow for a view of the
badlands beyond. It got its name from the fact that it had been
built into the framework of the Periphery, which helped to
give the restaurant a very large, and highly unusual space.
The ceiling, for instance, was not quite nine feet high on one
end and well over twelve feet on the other.

Normally the busy time was in the evening, when the
back room would be filled with couples looking for a romantic

dinner that wasn't prohibitively expensive. The lunchtime crowd was generally light but regular. Today, however, was different.

"Jesus H. Christ!" Phil exclaimed as they came through the door. "Who got shot this time?"

Indeed, not only were the tables full, but the patrons sitting down were sharing their tables with those forced to eat standing up. It was so crowded, the waitresses could barely get through with the food. It was a minor miracle that one waitress did, in fact, notice the four new arrivals standing by the door.

"What's the occasion?" Dr. Peris asked her.

"Total chaos. We've got the Devil with us," she explained. "If you're brave, there's actually plenty of seats in the back, but nobody wants to sit in the same room with 'em."

"Well, well, well! Even Lucifer comes here," Phil quipped.

"I only wish that were true." The waitress gave Dr. Nielsen a brief smile as she handed out the menus. "But it's the other kind of Devil, I'm afraid. If you want to risk it, feel free to go in there. I'll be back 'round in a few minutes to get your orders."

Next instant she was gone, swallowed up by the crowd.

"So." Phil turned to the others. "Care to sit in the Infernal section?"

"That's the smoking lounge, I presume?"

"I Suppose we could go to Minka's," Dr. Peris suggested, half-heartedly. Being a native Titanian, he was taking the news with far more consternation than the Newcomers.

As for Carlina, something else was occurring to her.

Of course! Serena must have meant star-devils!

"C'mon, I'm starving."

Without even checking to see if the others were following, she pushed her way through the crowd and on into the back room.

Sitting at a prime table in front of the windows, were two men, one dark-haired and the other blonde. They looked like most vytoc, tall, pale, and slender, but they were wearing dark glasses, which wrapped around their heads, concealing their eyes completely. More ominous were the large handguns they wore in shoulder holsters and the long daggers on their belts. A pair of dark overcoats lay folded over a neighbouring chair.

"Never thought they existed," Dr. Peris whispered.

"I've heard," Phil added in a more normal tone of voice. "That they're just actors. Perfectly normal humans dressed up like the KGB to scare the plebs into obedience."

"How to you account for the crystals, then?"

"Make-up. Hollywood does it all the time, back home. Of course, nobody's gonna get close enough to tell one way or another."

"They say their eyes glow red."

"Or green and purple for all you know. With those glasses on, it's all up to your imagination anyhow."

"Well, then. Perhaps you should go over there," said Dr. Peris, incredulously. "Knock their glasses off. See if it's true."

"Not with those guns on, baby," Phil smiled at him. "I'm not whuppin' on anyone packing heat, human or not."

As she had promised, the waitress came by a few minutes later.

"Decided to be the brave ones after all," she said, pulling out her compustylus and order pad. "So, what'll it be today?"

Phil jerked a thumb towards the other table.

"Out of curiosity, what are they having?"

"Soup and cider, mostly," the waitress shrugged. "We don't usually get their kind. But we've got mashed turnips and Charlie's whipping up some lemon cream, so that should hold 'em. Appears they're here for the cider at any rate. They've already drunk four jugs as it is."

"So it's true they don't eat solid food?"

"Blood and virgin's tears is the usual story," she said. "But here it's soup and cider, so that's what we give 'em."

"Good. I'll have what they're having: blood and virgin's tears!"

"That'll be the tomato soup with turnips, then," the waitress said, rolling her eyes. "And for the rest of you?"

The other doctors decided to order something a bit more substantial, namely mechelbread sandwiches, though Nigel decided to have a bowl of the soup as well.

Carlina waited until the waitress had gone back into the crowded front room before getting up from the table. It was now or never.

"'Lina?"

"Where's she goin'?"

"Dr. White, are you insane?"

Approaching the other table, she was surprised to see both men stand up to greet her.

"Oh, you don't need to..."

The dark-haired vytoc gave her a slight bow.

"It is customary for gentlemen to stand at the approach of a beautiful woman," he said. "You are Dr. White I presume -- Ja? You may call me Dr. Trug. My companion is Mr. Martyn. How might we be of service to you?"

He motioned toward a free chair but she preferred to remain standing as the star-devils took their seats.

"I...I need to make a petition."

"A petition? Surely that is ein matter for the Liaison Office?"

"I tried the Liaison Office, but Mr. Géricault...wouldn't help me. It's about my sister, you see, Christina Manning. She was among those arrested at the University this morning."

"An official arrest is it? I see your problem. Do you know the charge?"

"It's my understanding she started a food fight in the cafeteria."

The vytoc burst into laughter.

"Himmel! The youth these days!" Dr. Trug gasped. "Such gross criminal conduct!"

"It seems there was a Facilitator involved."

"Ja, ja, very serious. A vytoc cornered by young people armed with rotten tomatoes. Obviously, another assassination attempt."

"They'll throw the book at them for certain," Mr. Martyn added. "I'm surprised they didn't call us in."

Carlina wasn't quite sure what he meant by that last statement, but you always heard rumours about star-devils working for the Security Services.

"Will you help me?" She pleaded.

"My lady, I cannot guarantee results," Dr. Trug told her. "But I do promise I will investigate the matter and, if there is no better reason for your sister to be in custody, I will make certain that she is freed. You have my word."

"Thank you, Doctor. Thank you very much."

"Of course," Phil said as Carlina returned to her seat. "The Devil's word isn't worth much, you know. And that goes double for the Gestapo."

"For who?"

"He means they're German," Nigel explained. "Back on Earth (and it's been a while, mind you, when I was a lad) the Germans tried to take over the world, and met with some success. The Gestapo were the ones who kept the order once their army had done its bit. Needless to say, they weren't much for kindness and compassion."

"Brass knuckles on an iron fist," Phil added. "I can see why you guys call 'em devils."

Dr. Peris gave Carlina a confused look. She just shook her head.

"Newcomers. Don't try to understand them. It only gets worse when they try to explain."

"Got shipped all the way up to bleeding Scotland when they blitzed London," Nigel was saying. "My father had an old friend who owned a small farm and he thought we'd be safer out in the country. Nothing unusual there, of course. Lots of children were being sent away. Only he forgot to mention to my brother and me, that said farm was located north of Glasgow. Longest train ride of my life! Ah, here comes our food."

"Yes! Blood and virgin's tears! My favourite!"

"Poking the lion, Albert?" Nigel gave a quick look behind him, but the star devils didn't seem to be paying them any mind.

"Kicking at krauts is more like it."

In the near-empty room, one did not have to speak very loudly to be heard, but Phil was speaking loud enough to be heard in the kitchen. It would be impossible for the star-devils not to overhear. His companions stared at him, appalled, except for Nigel, who simply looked annoyed. Still, his designated targets continued to ignore him.

"Y'know," Phil continued in his drill-instructor tone of voice. "Krauts are rather famous for their rocketry. Wonder if they've got a rocketport somewhere around here?"

"Phil, really!"

"I'm serious! Laas even said that if there was a spaceport, it'd be guarded by the Devil himself. And there they are! I'll bet..." But his words broke off as a pale hand gripped him firmly on the shoulder.

"Und how is das blut today?" Dr. Trug asked. "I believe the special was AB negative."

"Yeah, great. Tastes like tomatoes," Phil said, giving Dr. Trug a sideways look. "So, you gonna spring her sister or what?"

"That remains to be seen. In the meantime, should you wish to experiment further with vytoc cuisine, you might begin with this. We much prefer it to blood or, for that matter, tears."

He pulled a small box from his coat and set it on the table in front of Dr. Nielsen.

"Auf Wiedersehen!"

Phil just stared at the box.

"Tapioca," he read. "I insult them and they give me a box of instant pudding."

"So?"

"Wonder what I'd have to say to 'em to get butterscotch?"

Chapter Six

For Christina, it had been a long, strange afternoon.

She lay on what had to be the hardest bed in the world, in what looked like a hospital room...and a sparsely furnished hospital room at that. It lacked a communicator, television, game player -- or even a book to read. There was nothing for her to do but stare at the ceiling, ruminate over the events of the morning, and try to ignore the growing apprehension that she might not be out in time for tonight's rehearsals.

The drive down had been easy enough. The arresting agent remained civil, but then, they *did* have the Cat in the van with them. There seemed to be some argument as to their destination, though. The agents kept telling the Cat they should "take it home," but the Cat disagreed. He snapped at them in a language Christina didn't understand, but the agents must have known what he was saying – it ended the argument, anyway.

She was brought to Tower 4, Titan City's courthouse and legal services building, and escorted through the main police department entrance on level 45. Although Christina had been to this tower once before, to give evidence at Cassandra's inquest, she had never been below the level 70 criminal courts. To be honest, she'd never been lower than the Discount Shopping Center on Flat 55. Just being in the 40's was a new and terrifying experience.

Her school satchel, and everything in it, had been left in the reading room. (Hopefully, Lyndsi had thought to pick it up and was keeping it safe.) But the lady at the police desk showed little concern over the fact that she couldn't show ID. However, she *did* make a point of taking Christina's picture -- not to mention all of her bracelets and hair combs as well.

Then came the pat down and a body scan, but that was the worst of it. They never made her change out of her clothes. Proof, she supposed, that she wasn't being charged with anything. So why was she still here?

Her memory flitted back to the first interrogation: she had been put in one of those small rooms that have only one chair and the single light that always shines in your eyes. The Cat had come in, looking like one of the Facilitators in *Tower Eighteen.* But the aura of menace was brief, if it was felt at all. He never touched her -- or even threatened her. In fact, he didn't do much of anything except lean against the wall and ask questions:

"Been at University long?"

"No. This is my first semester."

"Have you heard any rumours of Resistance activity, or has anyone confided in you with regards to such activity?"

"No."

"Can you think of a reason why someone might want to keep firearms in a dormitory?"

"It's an engineering school," she said with a shrug. "Maybe they just wanted to find out how they work."

He seemed to like that answer.

"Do you know of a young man by the name of Silas Doering?"

"Yeah, a little. I mean, everybody knows Silas. But he's two years ahead of me, and he won't give freshmen time or tower."

"And what of Laurence Wittyn?"

"Real domestrutter. You always see him in the game room, topgoatin' the electrosoccer. Can't stand him. He thinks Newcomers are really star devils out of costume."

"Do you believe that?" Asked the Cat, stifling a laugh.

"Pul-ese! My sister married a Newcomer and he hates you just as much as anybody."

The Cat gave her an almost affectionate smile.

"I apologize for taking up your time, this morning," he said. "I'll have an agent come and give you some lunch and you can be on your way."

And that was the last she'd seen of him – or any vytoc, for that matter.

A pair of policemen showed up a few minutes later, but they weren't bringing her lunch. Instead, they took her to a holding room where she was put in with the dozen or so other women who had been arrested that morning.

They were not a pretty bunch. Six were "back-stairwell" girls, with thick make-up, and body paint, and very little in the way of clothing. Beside them sat several gang girls wearing leggings of rat-leather; their hair dyed in the colours of their affiliations.

Huddled in a far corner was a pale young woman with red-orange hair. She wore soapstone sandals and a rough, meschel-fibre dress, which hung loose on her gaunt frame. She was painfully thin, except for her abdomen, which was swollen in what Christina guessed to be the second trimester of pregnancy.

And she stank like a backed up sewer. But being that she was also the least threatening person in the cell, Christina chose to sit next to her anyway.

"Hi! I'm Christina."

"Terisia," the pregnant woman said, her voice monotone.

"So. What are you in for?"

"Theft. Got caught in CyTrue's produce, stealing tangerines."

"Why – what happened? Someone steal your ration cards?"

"Not everyone gets rations, tower child," chided a girl with blue hair.

"But she's a mother!" In Christina's world, special rations were always given to pregnant women. Carlina had received them twice now: they came in a purple envelope, and entitled the new mother to extra grain, greens, and citrus fruit.

"Some mothers is more important than others."

"Due sometime next year," Terisia said, patting her bulge. "With luck, it won't be a boy."

"Teris, you'd better just shoot yourself in the stomach first chance you get," snarled the blue-haired girl. "Boy or girl, that kid's already dead and you know it."

"No, Whips, there's a chance now." Terisia gave Christina a slight smile. "Took me six tries and the CyTrue's on 85, but I got in at last. We'll be safe now."

"Whu...you mean, you were *trying* to get arrested?"

Even now, she could hear the gang girls laughing at her.

"Confessed to twelve counts of taking tangerines, bread, eggs, and spinach," Terisia said, proudly. "It should get me at least six years, if not eight. The prison takes care of the babies, see. And when I get out, my little one will be healthy and strong -- and maybe he can run...."Her voice fell away.

"Run where?"

"Get away from his father."

But Christina would never find out what threat was posed by the unborn child's father. Before Terisia could explain, the cell door opened and a pair of Security men walked in.

"Christina Manning? Come with us."

And she was off again, for another escorted journey

through the grey, undecorated halls of justice. She still felt a glimmer of hope. After all, the Cat himself had promised she'd be released. But the agents weren't taking her to the entrance level. Instead, they led her down to level 42 and through the walkway leading to what Titanians call the "Black Tower."

In actuality, the skyscraper was brownish-grey rather than black, and at only 98 stories, rather unimposing by Titan standards. But it *was* the headquarters for all Facilitator activity in Titan City, housing the Security Services, Prefecture, and the Liaison Office. It wouldn't do to simply call it an administrative tower.

The Black Tower stood alone, with its only connectors being the entrance at Flat 95, the parking zone ramps, and the walkway to Tower 4. It was the latter that did the most to give the building its dark reputation. Enter at level 42, it was said, and you may never see the curve of the dome again.

Not a happy thought.

Christina was again brought into an interrogation room, and again, she had to sit in the lone chair with the light in her eyes. This time, however, it was a human agent doing the questioning. He said his name was Alrund and that he had special authority within the Security Services. That had struck her as odd, considering the Cat had already questioned her. Surely, *he* wouldn't be outranked by a mere human?

"You are Christina Saline Manning, sister to Cassandra Lynn?"

"Yeah."

"You're familiar with a man by the name of Daniel Cawthorn?"

"Used to, but that was a long time ago. He ran off when Cass died."

"You know where he's hiding." It wasn't a question.

"No idea," she said, growing irritated. "He's in hiding, you know. He didn't exactly tell us the address."

"Where is he, Christina?"

"How would I know?"

"I think you know very well."

"Sheesh! I was arrested for a food fight, fercryingoutloud!"

"You were arrested because you know the whereabouts of Daniel Cawthorn. Now tell me – where is he?"

"You're going up the *wrong* rampway, Green Bean! Look, can I talk to the Cat..."

"I'm asking the questions here," he said, cutting her off and standing very close. They were practically nose-to-nose.

"Daniel Cawthorn. Your sister, Cassandra, was very close to him was she not?"

"Yeah."

"And your other sister, Carlina, supports him."

"No way! We haven't heard from him since Cass was killed!"

"Do not cover for her! We know your family supports Daniel Cawthorn! Where do the transfers take place?"

"I don't know – bank, maybe?"

"There are no banks involved, Christina. This is a matter of ration fraud and it is very serious. Could there be a family friend aiding in the transfers? Someone who's familiar with the lower levels of the city, perhaps? Like Dr. Nielsen?"

"Snurrgles! You gotta stay inside the dome, Bean! The bad air's affecting your brain."

"Christina..."

"We don't know where he is, all right!"

And so it went for at least an hour, though it felt longer. Agent Alrund continued to ask the same stupid questions over and over, while refusing to listen to anything Christina told him. Though, to tell the truth, the only thing she knew about Daniel Cawthorn was that the ghost children had been hiding him. Gaila might know something, but Christina had no intention of telling him about *her*.

Mercifully, he was called away, but not before giving Christina a couple slaps across the face. She gingerly felt the growing bruise under her right eye. Fortunately, *Wider Horizons* wouldn't be opening for another week yet. A little theatre make-up should take care of it until then.

So far, that had been the worst of it. Some other agent had put her into this hospital room and here she'd been for the past two, maybe three hours.

And still no lunch!

Bored. Bored. Bored! She got up from the bed to stare dejectedly out the window. In any given episode of *Tower Eighteen,* Pym Davis would either be infiltrating or escaping the Black Tower. And any attempt to imprison him would be foiled within the hour.

Of course, he somehow managed to keep a rope handy.

With a grappling hook!

And he knew how to get the windows open.

And he usually got an outside room, allowing him to swing across to another building.

"Schnuurrgles!" Christina moaned, staring into the light well. Was she *ever* going to get out of here?

With nothing better to do, she began running through her lines for *Wider Horizons.* It would have been better if she'd had her script with her but -- what the hell -- improvisation is the heart of the theatre.

"Let's see...fourth act, scene three. Lynessa has just found out that Vyn is about to stage his coup against the Latebran Council, possibly getting killed in the process ... and she makes one last attempt at turning his mind:

"Fine! Go then!" She said to a chair. "Point a gun at the Devil and think it'll do you any good! Can't you face reality? They'll kill you! Or if they don't, they'll think of something worse. They're very good at worse. Do you want to end up like Masie? Or perhaps like poor Wyllum?"

Then she jumped up on the chair, turning to face the spot where she'd been standing.

"So, Vyn says it doesn't matter. Wyllum's sacrifice was not in vain and he must make a statement for human dignity if not freedom itself. Yabba, yabba. An' he's gonna carry her to the farthest star, away from the demon's reach. Yabba, yabba, yabba, and so on!"

She jumped back to her original place in front of the chair to continue as Lynessa. This meant she now had her back to the door. And she was so thoroughly engrossed in the scene, she didn't notice that the door was opening.

"Oh, no! Not me!" she shouted at the chair. "I'm not Wyllum, trotting off to his death for a tripple of pretty words. The demon has control because he has power. And we are nothing to that power. Fight them and you are dead!"

"Ach! But how the demon *fears* the comfortable chair!"

"Whutthe...?" Christina made a sudden jump, spinning half-way round in mid air.

Standing behind her was a tall, dark-haired man wearing dark glasses and a long, dark coat. Instinctively, she tried to make a break for it, her legs making a sudden move to the right -- but the chair was in the way. She tripped, pitched sideways, and ended up sitting in it, one leg dangling over the armrest.

"Who the hell are you?"

"You cannot tell? I would think it obvious."

"I'm not a virgin!"

"That still leaves blood," said the star-devil, smiling. "But I promise, I am not here to harm you. Your sister, you see, has made a deal with the Devil to hasten your release. I am here as Mephistopheles, but you may call me Dr. Trug."

"You're gonna get me out of here?"

Dr. Trug tossed her the small parcel containing her bracelets and hair accessories taken by the Police.

"The door is open, my Lady."

"Top Floor!"

In a shot, Christina was out and running down the corridor. She didn't quite know where she was going, but most of Titan's towers were built around a central core, where the main verticals would be located. Barring that, there'd always be stairwells in the corners.

"You'll want to turn left at the next intersection," came a voice from behind her. "The verticals will be on your right."

She stopped and turned as Dr. Trug trotted up to her.

"You're not following me, are you?"

"Just until you have left the building. After that, you are on your own."

"Good," she said, turning down the next corridor. "'Cause a guy like you could seriously cramp my social level. Is it true your eyes glow red?"

"Actually, at the moment they are green."

"You mean like...whoa!"

Dr. Trug had pulled his glasses up just long enough for Christina to get a good glimpse. His eyes looked glassy, like marbles, but with a soft internal glow. As she watched, they turned from a bright jade to a yellowish lime green.

"Queerd! But why bother with the glasses? Green may not be as evil-looking as red but it still gets attention."

"The colour changes with mood," Dr. Trug explained, smugly. "And I would prefer other people not to know how I am feeling."

"Makes sense," she shrugged as they approached the verticals. "So, what level we goin' to?"

Her question was answered by the vertical. The moment they stepped inside, the destination readout began flashing '95.'

"Wish I could do that," she said, half to herself.

"If I were you," Dr. Trug replied. "I would be very careful about saying such things in the presence of vytoc. Someone could get the wrong impression."

"Why? Is that what happened to Cassi?"

The star-devil gave a sigh.

"You sister was a very human young woman," he told her. "Which, I fear, was more than some people could tolerate."

At the opening of the doors, he dropped the subject.

"Go to your right, then turn left down the next

corridor. That will lead to the reception area."

"Thanks Doc!" Christina said, over her shoulder. "You're a saint!"

Her ears told her that the star-devil was still behind her, but she didn't care. She was free now! As she turned the corner, she could see the windows of the Black Tower's atrium ahead of her.

She almost ran over the man coming up the hall. As she passed, he caught her by the arm, nearly lifting her off her feet as he pulled her back.

"What are you doing up here?" He demanded. To her horror, she realized he was another vytoc.

"She's being released. Let her go!" Dr. Trug shouted from down the hall.

"By whose authority?"

"Mein!"

"That's not applicable! She is here under the protection of the Liaison Office..."

But by that point, Dr. Trug had caught up to them, and he was in no mood to argue or, for that matter, let the other vytoc finish speaking. Without a word, he wrenched the Facilitator's hand from her arm.

"Run. *Schnell!*"

He didn't need to say it twice. Christina bolted for the entrance.

"Get back here!"

The other vytoc tried to grab her again, but Dr. Trug pulled him back by his shirt collar. Glancing backward, Christina caught the gleam of light on metal. A moment later, and the other vytoc was stumbling down the hall, clutching his stomach.

I did not see that! Her thoughts screamed in her head. *I did not just see a star-devil stab a Facilitator!*

She did not stop running until she was nearly to the hospital.

But there was no sense in going in. By now, Carlina was most likely home with the kids. Best thing to do would be to head back to the dorms and see if Lyndsi had her satchel, and maybe get a CytriSuds from the canteen.

Stumbling towards the big, public verticals by the immediate care entrance, the Facilitator's words continued to echo in her mind.

So, she hadn't been a prisoner of the Security Services after all!

But the Liaison office? Did *Mr. Géricault* have her arrested?

They're looking for Daniel Cawthorn, she thought, absent-mindedly touching her bruised cheek. Obviously, this had something to do with Cassandra, but as for what or why?

She wished she knew.

Chapter Seven

"Lemme see! Lemme see!"

"All right, already," Dr. Nielsen laughed, adjusting the microscope. He stepped back as Serena eagerly jumped up to look through the eyepiece.

"Wow! That's my blood?"

"That it is. Those little dots you see are your red blood cells and those large purple ones..."

"Leukocytes!"

"Are leukocytes, yeah. So now, Miss Smartypants, tell me what the red ones are called."

"Erythrocytes! Ha! Didn't think I knew that one, didja!"

"Should've know better, shouldn't I."

And, indeed, he should have. After years of working in paediatric cancer wards, Phil was already well aware of the penchant small children have for big words. Plenty of times he'd met with a patient who looked barely out of kindergarten. And while he'd be trying to explain things in the simplest and gentlest possible terms, the kid would invariably answer back using all the medical jargon. The simple and gentle language, he'd learned, was best saved for the parents.

Then there was Serena, who may not have cancer, but who lived her life in a hospital anyway. However, this proximity was proving to be a godsend for Phil as he tried to learn more about the regenerative effects of vytasynene. In this, the girl was a perfectly willing guinea pig, just so long as she got to use the equipment.

"Now, what I'm finding curious," he said, transferring the image to the computer screen. "Are these light coloured cells here."

He focused in on a cluster of cells. They were the size and shape of the red blood cells but didn't appear to possess haemoglobin.

"Probably the Type II Erythrocytes," Serena said, matter-of-factly. "Ghost child blood."

"You have secondary blood cells?"

"Yeah. They do the same thing as the red blood, but different."

Phil was quiet for a moment as he looked at the cells. Part of him was wondering what her bone marrow looked like, whereas his other thoughts were travelling down a much darker road.

"Do they use vytasynene to make vytoc, I wonder?"

"No," Serena answered. "But there's an old story that goes around about how it was supposed to make a kind of half-vytoc – or maybe soften people up so they'd agree to become the real thing."

"Always trying to get a volunteer," Phil said into his microscope. "Sure as hell wish they'd leave Carlina alone."

"Yeah. Mr. Gerry's still in love with Cassi."

"So I've heard."

"Which is stupid since he killed her."

"Hold it! He what?!"

Serena smiled up at him, smugly.

"Nobody likes to talk about it, but Danny Cawthorn was trying to get her to refuse – going through the change -- you know. The story is that Gerry tried to shoot him, but Cassandra got in the way ... or that's what Danny says, anyway."

She started to say something else, but was interrupted by a shrill beeping sound coming from a watch-like device she wore on her wrist. Without even looking at the readout, she slammed her other hand down on the reset button.

"Schnurrgles! Back in a moment – gotta dose."

"I take it your mom has your supply?"

"Nah, I've got a day's worth with me. It's just that it's not polite..."

"I am a doctor, you know. Needles don't exactly scare me."

"Yeah...guess so. As long as you don't mind." She pulled a thin box from a pocket inside her pinafore.

"Actually, I'm a little curious," Phil said. "You need a shot every nine hours, correct?"

"For grown-ups it is. I'm at every six and for the babies, it's a dose every two."

Serena took out a syringe and a vial of thick, shimmering liquid. In the fluorescent lighting, it seemed to glow slightly, like phosphorescent mercury.

"Don't you need a tourniquet?"

"I know where my veins are."

In one quick, fluid motion, Serena inserted the needle into her arm and pushed in the plunger. Then, to Phil's surprise, she returned the syringe to its box. He noticed a red line drawn on one end. The needle of the used syringe faced towards the line, whereas a second, unused syringe, faced away.

"You save your needles?"

"We don't get much re-supply," Serena explained, returning the box to her pocket. "Everyone gets issued a set number of needles and a sterilizer. You have to clean and sterilize your needles every night and there's *no sharing*."

She said this in the sing-song manner of a child repeating something that had been drilled into her head over and over by countless adults.

"World's cleanest junkies," Phil said, bemused.

"Better than the other kind. We get lots of 'em on the street – an' I'd rather be a ghost child than one of *them*."

"You guys live all the way down on street level?"

"Below it."

Phil raised an eyebrow. "Isn't that a rather rough neighbourhood?"

"It's mean," Serena agreed with a shrug. "Lot's of people killing each other over stupid stuff. They know better than to mess with us, though."

"Afraid of the drug?"

"Afraid of the dart guns," she said. "Death is the only thing anybody respects down there. An' our guns give 'em something worse'n death – so they leave us alone."

Phil gave a low whistle.

"And I thought south-side was bad." He pulled the slide from the microscope. "Now, I've managed to isolate a few of these 'type II' erythrocytes of yours. Let's see how they look under the electron microscope, and then we'll begin the chemical analysis."

But for once, Serena wasn't acting excited. She wasn't even looking at him. Instead, she was focused intently on the laboratory door.

To his surprise, Mr. Port came into the room. Odd. For some reason, he'd expected to see Mr. Géricault.

"Dr. Nielsen! Nice to see you've settled in all right. A citizen by now, I take it?"

"Uh, yeah. So what brings..."

"I don't suppose Dr. White is available?"

"He's actually at an autopsy right now. I could give him a message if you'd like."

"Splendid," Mr. Port brightened in his weasel-like way. "Do tell Dr. White he is needed at the Liaison Office at no later than 16 hours today. It is a matter of extreme importance."

"Will do."

"Excellent! And a good day to you!"

And then he was gone. Serena stuck her tongue out at the door.

"Good riddance."

"Don't like vytoc, do you," Phil grinned.

"Don't like Facilitators. Vytoc are all right."

"Okay, I'll bite. What's the difference?"

"Facilitators run Latebra."

"And vytoc don't?"

"Good vytoc don't."

"That's a contradiction in terms, ya'know."

"Nobody's all bad," Serena giggled. "But you gotta watch 'em if they've gots control."

But the whole world? Phil had never thought about what kind of influence the vytoc might have outside of Titan's dome. From what he'd heard, Tylerville and the agro-colonies operated free of vytoc "facilitation." But if you thought about it, there wasn't much to prevent them from doing whatever they wished, *wherever* they wished.

He thought back to the mysterious, unnamed roadway. Perhaps Laas could clue him in on the drive next Monday.

Meanwhile, Serena's opinion of Mr. Port was more than shared by Nigel, when he returned to the lab half an hour later. He was considerably less than thrilled to hear about his "extremely important" appointment with the Liaison Office.

"He didn't say why they wanted to see me?"

"Nope."

"So, there's an afternoon shot to hell. By the way, I got to talking with Dr. Morton about your subject 56 and his regenerating spleen."

"And?"

"It seems you diagnosis was correct. While your subject may have had leukaemia, it did not kill him."

"It didn't?"

"No. As it turns out, he was shot to death."

Chapter Eight

"They're into the pantry supplies again," complained Mr. Géricault, tossing a handful of pudding boxes onto Kittyvoc's desk.

The head of security just looked at them and shrugged.

"Typical linewalker prank," he said, turning back to his computer screen.

"And since when did you become so tolerant of linewalker pranks?"

"I like tapioca."

"Well some of us don't and ... what is so amusing, may I ask?"

"It's rather the point, isn't it?" Kittyvoc smiled. "That you don't like tapioca."

He began leafing through a pile of reports, making a point not to look at the man hovering over him.

"If you must know," he said. "They're protesting Coriolon's banishment."

"With pudding?"

"You'd rather they shoot you?"

"They've already stabbed Portysanon!"

Kittyvoc reached into a drawer and pulled out a roll of duct tape. It hit the desktop with a dull thud.

"You are not taking this seriously."

"Portysanon knows what happens when you get in a linewalker's way," Kittyvoc replied. "It's not my fault if he cannot use common sense."

"And what about you," grumbled Mr. Géricault. "I'd say common sense should tell you these degenerates are a threat to law and order!"

"Yet, funny how these degenerates were invited by the police, of all people, to aid in a murder investigation. And, aside from yours, I haven't heard a single complaint."

Mr. Géricault turned his head toward the ceiling as though asking supplication from God.

"Gooch!"

"Senior Detective Gooch," Kittyvoc pointed out. "Has long been a friend of the Security Services. If he feels the linewalkers could be of help, *and* if said linewalkers prove willing, then I seen no reason to stand in the way."

"Besides," he added. "He was on very good terms with Coriolon, who is still one of our best recruiters. Had you allowed him to stay on, you just might have found yourself with that new vytoc you've been longing for."

"Another linewalker, in other words," groused Mr. Géricault. "Well, we do not need another linewalker. We have more than enough of those as it is and two too many in Titan City."

"Fine then," Kittyvoc sighed. "I'll tell Talonyvoc when he reports in. But that takes Fosteperon off the assassination probe."

"You don't have any humans that could do it?" Mr. Géricault asked. "What about Lewys? He's a good man."

Kittyvoc's eyes narrowed ever so slightly.

"I'd prefer a vytoc on that probe," he said. "There might be shooting."

"Whatever works, then. Just be sure to send les bosches back where they came from."

"I'll tell them Trois-Rivieres is lovely this time of year."

"So long as they're gone."

Kittyvoc's cold demeanour was anything but reassuring, but Mr. Géricault knew better than to press the matter. The man had, after all, spent his human years among the Chetnik partisans, fighting both the Germans and the Russians, as well as his fellow Serbs, during the latest European war. In contrast, Mr. Géricault had never been in anything worse than a tavern brawl. But even back then, he knew never to pick a fight with a soldier. Sullenly, he walked through the finely decorated public levels of the Black Tower; back to his office on the uppermost floor.

It did not help to find it already occupied.

At this point, it should be made clear that Mr. Géricault's name wasn't actually "Géricault." His given name had been Gerard Roquette, but upon his transference from human to vytoc, he had taken on another identity and with it, the name, Gerysalon. "Géricault" was simply a moniker he liked to use among the lesser humans, who found vytoc names unwieldy at best. To the people who mattered, his own people, he was always Gerysalon.

Subsequently, the man currently sitting behind the desk with his boots on the blotter might call himself "Dr. Trug," but Gerysalon knew him better as the linewalker, Talonyvoc.

Talonyvoc, quite relaxed, was enjoying a particularly large bowl of tapioca pudding.

"Get out of here!"

"Et un *bon* après-midi à vous aussi, monsieur," said Talonyvoc, getting up and casually moving to a chair on the other side of the desk. Once settled, he put his feet up again, taking care to kick over Gerysalon's GÉRICAULT nameplate.

"I've already spoken with Kittyvoc," Gerysalon said, taking the freshly vacated seat. "You are to leave immediately."

"And without a single apology for the inconvenience, I'm sure."

"Yours or mine?"

"Interesting choice of words," Talonyvoc said, twirling his spoon. "Is there something about our investigation that upsets you?"

"Linewalkers sticking their noses where they are not wanted upsets me. We do not need your kind interfering in police matters."

"Ironic, considering it was the police who asked for our help in the first place. Which brings us to the matter of the girl today..."

"Get out!"

"Wrong answer!" Talonyvoc said, cheerfully. "It seems she's related to Cassandra Manning, whose murder – interestingly enough -- Coriolon was investigating when he was so unceremoniously sent packing."

"That has nothing to do with anything," huffed Gerysalon. "The girl caused a disturbance at the University and might have links to the Resistance. That Cassandra was her sister is just a coincidence."

"Mon ami, I do not believe in coincidences."

"It's a small city, Talon. These things happen."

Impatiently, Gerysalon stood up again. Throwing a linewalker bodily from a room is not a recommended action even for a soldier like Kittyvoc. But right now, he was ready to risk even certain injury to get the man out of there. As luck would have it, his communicator chimed before he could take the matter farther.

It was the receptionist.

"Géricault here. What is it?"

"A Dr. White to see you sir. He says he has an appointment at 16."

"Of course. Tell him to wait a moment. I'm almost

done here."

"Understood, sir."

"Feeling ill?" Talonyvoc asked, innocently.

"My business with Dr. White is no business of yours."

"Now this Dr. White," Talonyvoc said. "Wouldn't happen to be the same Dr. White who's married to *another* Dr. White --maiden name, Manning-- who just *happens* to be the sister of Christina Manning, and therefore, also the sister of Cassandra Manning ... ja?"

"You are dismissed, Talonyvoc!"

"Am I to assume this is yet another coincidence?! Will there be others? Have we yet to exhaust the supply of Manning sisterhood?"

"Leave!"

"If you so insist."

With a swish of his coattails, Talonyvoc was up and out the door.

"You could at least..."

"Servus!"

"...take your dish!"

But the linewalker was already gone. Gerysalon heard the click of the door lock activating. With a curse, he unlocked it again.

Bosch!

He took Talonyvoc's empty bowl and set it inside one of the drawers of the richly carved armoire which served as his wet bar. Cursing in both French and English, he pulled out the several boxes of tapioca pudding that had been placed among the bottles. These joined the bowl in the lower drawer.

There were a few more choice words spoken when he checked his liquor supply.

His new bottle of Chambord was half-drained, and the rum was nearly empty. A small flask of peach schnapps was missing entirely. He could safely assume it was currently taking up the pocket space made empty by the boxes of pudding.

Linewalkers!

Back at his desk, he reset his nameplate and neatened up the other various items Talonyvoc had kicked aside. Finally, when he was certain everything was in its proper place, he activated the communicator.

"You may tell Dr. White he can come up now."

But Dr. White, it seemed, knew how to play the game as well. It was another ten minutes before he finally came through the door.

"Hello, Doctor!" Gerysalon exclaimed, as though greeting an old friend. "How good of you to come on such short notice."

He motioned towards the chair formerly occupied by Talonyvoc and opened up the bar.

"Would you care for a cognac? Or perhaps a gin and tonic?"

"None for me, thanks," said Dr. White with chilled politeness. "I stopped drinking eight years ago."

"The offer remains," Gerysalon said, pouring a brandy for himself and ignoring the connotations behind that last remark.

He returned to his desk, giving Dr. White his best politician's smile. It wasn't having much effect. Your typical dour Englishman, Dr. White was wearing a scowl that would make Churchill appear light-hearted in comparison.

Until now, Gerysalon had never seen the man up close. Dr. White had the usual Anglo-Saxon face: round but slightly elongated, like a balloon. Hazel eyes were framed with nascent crows feet, and his light brown hair was in rapid retreat from his forehead. Add the lopsided shoulders, permanently hunched from too many years of looking into microscopes, and the end result was far from impressive. What Carlina saw in the man, he had no idea.

"As I'm sure you've heard," he said, pulling a dossier from a pile beside him. "Dr. Peris will be retiring later this Spring. Your name is among those in consideration to be his replacement."

"It has been my understanding that Dr. Spaulding would be the new head, given that he is next in seniority," Dr. White answered.

"He is the favoured candidate, yes. But that hardly guarantees him the job."

"I'd say he's the favoured candidate because he is the best man for the job."

"Well, that remains to be seen, doesn't it?"

"Dr. Arthur Spaulding should be the new head of research," Dr. White said firmly. "And I would appreciate it if you would withdraw my name from consideration."

"My dear Doctor!" Gerysalon exclaimed. "What has happened to your ambition? Are you really the same Dr. White who once sought admittance to the Royal College of Physicians?"

"How did you...yes, of course. Mr. Port."

"He is very thorough."

"I'm sure he is," said Dr. White sullenly. "But let us just say my priorities have changed in the last eight years. I'm quite happy to be where I am."

"On level 86," noted Gerysalon. "You could be much higher."

"Where I live is none of your concern," countered Dr. White. "And whatever the future may bring, I do not need a *Facilitator* to aid me in any way."

"It isn't all about you."

"No. Of course it isn't." Dr. White was simmering with rage. "Carlina told me you had been around this morning. And, by the way, you may have this back."

He pulled a bag of macaroni from his work satchel and threw it on the desk.

"Are you sure you want to do that," Gerysalon said, evenly. "Macaroni with cheese is very popular with children."

"Just. Leave us. Alone."

"You know I cannot do that. Carlina is needed for a greater purpose..."

"Oh, bugger your greater purpose," Dr. White said, testily getting to his feet. "You've already taken one woman away from me. I'll be damned if I'll let you take another! And no amount of bribery is going to change my mind! Good day, Mister Géricault!"

"The position remains open should you reconsider."

A heartfelt slam of the door was Dr. White's reply.

"You will regret that decision, I assure you," Gerysalon said to the door.

Sipping his brandy, he turned his chair around to gaze out the window. From here he could see the wide mall of flat 95, the skyscrapers towering on all sides like so many steel sequoias.

When he had first arrived on Terra Latebra, the dome was not yet complete; the human population still confined to the Old Colony. It had been a vytoc city then, and Gerysalon had helped to build it; finishing the dome and several of the taller towers with his own hands.

It was, he felt, a dream worthy of the greatest among men: a world where human and vytoc could live openly together, without all the secrecy that characterized their Earth-based concerns. But familiarity had done well to breed contempt, and finding decent initiates among the Latebrans had always been a challenge.

He remembered the excitement he'd felt when Taralkalon, his old foreman, told him a vytoc had been recruited from the Old Colony some decades prior. True, the man was just a Dutch sailor, not a true Latebran, but you had to start somewhere. He had sought out Coriolon in earnest, only to discover that Latebra's only vytoc had become a linewalker.

In time, he had managed to even the score a little with Portysanon. But Mr. Port wasn't a native either. He'd been born in Moscavide, near Lisbon.

Four hundred years of recruiting. *Four hundred!* And still they had yet to find a native Latebran willing to join in the Grand Matrix. Of course, it didn't help that the human population seemed determined to counteract any successes they might have in that direction. Cassandra had been one of the few souls brave enough to stand up to the societal pressure, but now... even she was gone.

But Cassandra's processing capsule was still ready and waiting. All he needed now was for Carlina to give consent and take her sister's place.

Always the damned consent!

It annoyed him that the Line Council, including their most *honoured* Lady, should be so particular about consent.

After all, does anyone ever truly know what he desires? In the long run, it was only a question of adaptation, anyway. Take an Earthman to Latebra and he'll grumble, but in the end, he'll assimilate. So why shouldn't a Latebran adapt just as easily to becoming a vytoc, whether he –or she-- originally wanted to be one or not?

The recruiting process? Beyond useless!

Finishing his drink, Gerysalon turned back to his desk. From one of the upper drawers, he pulled out a small box. In it was a hypodermic gun of a type used to subdue violent mental patients, and a vial of shimmering liquid.

He filled the hypo and set the dose to the smallest level possible. Then he set the gun on the desktop beside the bag of macaroni and just stared at it.

Tomorrow.

You could take lives or you could ruin them. Either way, he would convince Carlina to consent. And Dr. White (*both of them!*) was going to regret not taking him up on his offer.

Chapter Nine

The star-fish were not cooperating. For the sixth time, Carlina dipped the catcher into the murky, resin-filled tank. She moved it gently around, her spirits rising as she felt something struggle with the net. Hopeful, she pulled the wriggling creature to the surface, searching for the identifying jewel set into its carapace.

And the jewel was ... green.

"No, Emerald. Not you again!"

"Trying to catch Sapphire, aren't ya," chirped Serena, bounding over from the study table to the star-fish tank.

"He is the difficult one, yes."

"That's 'cause he wants you to sing for him first, like this!"

Serena whistled a tune and began quietly singing a "calling out" rhyme familiar among Titan's children:

"Saafire! Saafire! Swimming in the glup!

Saafire! Saafire! Won't you please come up!

The sun has ris'! A brand new day!

Is shining down the passageway!

Saafire! Saafire! Won't you come and play?"

A tentacled creature, about the size of a teapot, rose to the surface. Carlina was relieved to see it had a blue jewel set into its back.

"You're going to have to teach me that sometime," she said, trapping the star-fish in the catcher net and sliding it into a holding tank.

"You kinda hav'ta be a ghost child, I think," Serena said, running her arm through the resin. "Mom's tried it, but they don't respond the same way."

"You could play a flute," suggested Bull, her brother, still seated at the study table. "Muncie can get all three of 'em up just by playing *Sleep, My Dearie.*"

"Wonder if recorded music would work," Carlina mused as she drew a large syringe-full of translucent fluid from the creature. It only took her a moment, and soon Sapphire was sliding back into the murk with the others.

"At least that's finally out of the way," she said, recording the procedure on a chart attached to the tank. "Thank you, Serena."

The girl still had her arm deep in the resin.

"Uh, Carlina?"

"What?"

"I don't think we gots just three anymore."

She pulled something small and shiny out of the resin. It looked like a miniature version of Sapphire, but without the jewel.

"Top floor!" Bull cried, jumping up from the table to join his sister at the star-fish tank. "It looks just like a tocker crystal!"

He grabbed the little star-fish and held it at his throat.

"See? Just like a vytoc!"

"'Cept vytoc don't have tentacles!"

"Bet they could," Bull said, with all the enthusiasm of an eleven-year-old. "But they're inside! What if the Prefect was making a speech and a big 'ol tentacle came out of his mouth!"

"That's gross!"

"Here! Try it!" Bull thrust the wriggling creature at Serena's face.

"MOM!"

"All right, cool it you two," Carlina said, removing her protective gear. "Put it back and get cleaned up. In an hour, I'm going to be looking at those worksheets and they had better be completed."

"Yes, Doctor."

Reluctantly, Bull let the little star-fish slide back into the resin and together, he and his sister slumped off to the lavatories.

"What's going on?" Gaila asked, peering into the room. "I thought I heard a Mom-call."

"It was nothing," Carlina replied. "Just boys-will-be-boys-will-be-torments-to-their-sisters. A little preview of what I have to look forward to, I'm afraid."

"From what I've heard, Sophia's getting her hand in early," Gaila grinned, holding the door for Carlina.

"Sometimes, I wonder if she doesn't see an advantage in being the weaker child," Carlina said, glancing over at her daughter, sitting quietly in a corner. Sophia was busy playing with a set of 'Connect-O-Blocks.' She'd even figured out how to connect them, which was certainly a step in the right direction.

"She seems so helpless, but if she really wants something, she finds a way to get it. Yesterday, for instance, she managed to pull out the bottom desk drawer to get at a ball that'd rolled under there."

"Kid's not as dumb as she looks."

"I think she runs laps when my back is turned."

"Better turn our backs, then," kidded Gaila.

They set to work, running the star-fish blood through a network of tubing; combining it with carbon, nitrogen, and a mixture of phosphoproteins. The end result was a shimmering, phosphorescent liquid that looked like a translucent form of mercury.

Vytasynene.

Making it was illegal, but as withdrawal was fatal, a certain amount had to be produced to keep alive those already addicted. Their laboratory was authorized by the government and the women each received a stipend for their work. However, the entire project was kept strictly secret, listed in the city ledger as "Silicon Bio-Phosphate Research." The lab itself, was hidden away on the 60th level of the hospital tower, nowadays an unused area that had become a dumping ground for old equipment.

Should anyone ask, Carlina just said she worked on a

special government project Thursday nights.

She continued to bring Sophia along, as her daughter couldn't speak yet, but that naturally meant leaving "the lads" to fend for themselves. Thursday had thus become father-son night, almost always involving a trip to the children's museum and dinner somewhere greasy.

"Hey, Mom!"

Gaila started to look over her shoulder.

"What is it Sere...Ohmigod! What have you been doing!"

Carlina turned around just as Bull followed his sister into the lab. Both children were soaked to the skin – casualties of a lavatory water war.

"Our shirts had resin-glup on 'em."

"And your pants?"

"Them too."

"We heard one of the verticals open up," Bull said, speaking fast to head off the scolding. "Someone's coming!"

"Oh dear! Bull, take the cart and both of you get into the fish room and stay quiet. I'm setting the doors on code-lock."

"Understood!"

As the children hurried off with the cart full of processed vytasynene, Gaila had barely enough time to set the code on the auxiliary lab before the main door opened.

"Mr. Géricault?"

"Good evening, Doctors. I trust production is running smoothly." He held up a small canister. "I brought along a little something for the Ænoyc."[*]

"The wha...Oh, you mean the star-fish. Yes, they're in here." Gaila started to tap in the code when the door suddenly unlocked itself.

"That was a coded lock."

"I am aware of that."

Carlina gave Mr. Géricault a wary look as she followed him and Gaila into the other room. Serena and Bull took one look at the visitor and and bolted back into the main lab. They didn't go too far, though. Once or twice, Carlina caught a glimpse of white-blonde hair peeking out from around the doorway.

"You may have heard about the offer I made to your husband yesterday," Mr. Géricault was saying.

"As did most of the hospital and tower 10. He was quite furious."

"Still, the offer remains."

He shook a few granules from the canister into his hand; tossing them into the star-fish tank.

"A fellow vytoc once told me, that the reason humans resist us is because they see only the sharp edges, never the beauty of the facets. So, perhaps today, I can show you something of that beauty."

He began to hum a melody that was not so much sung

---

[*] Nearly impossible for a human being to pronounce, but ee-no'-ek comes close.

as emitted, the sound coming from his entire body and not just his mouth. It was a stirring, impassioned tune, of a sort that normally takes an entire symphony orchestra to create. Carlina almost found it enjoyable.

The star-fish were certainly enthralled. They surfaced and began to sing along. An odd little chorus of...

"Five!" Carlina exclaimed in amazement. "There's five now! And to think, last week we had only three."

"It does take about eighty years for them to reach sexual maturity," Mr. Géricault said, testily. "You'll no doubt have to separate the older ones from now on."

"Funny. We never could figure out how to sex them. We thought they were all male."

"They are hermaphroditic," explained Mr. Géricault. "In mating, they impregnate each other, which is why the young appear in pairs. Did you like the singing?"

"Singing? Oh, yes, the singing. We knew they responded to music but not quite like that."

"It is said that vytoc possess the music of the spheres."

"Forget it," Carlina said, cutting him off. After the business with Christina, she was in no mood for another proposition.

"You are needed to take up your sister's mantle."

"My family needs me far more than you do."

"Who said you had to leave your family?" Cajoled Mr. Géricault. "After all, this was why we created the colonies in the first place: so that humans and vytoc could live openly together. Join our Grand Matrix and your children will never want for anything."

"And what about my husband?" Countered Carlina. "According to Cass, physical relationships between vytoc and human beings are extremely hazardous – terminal even – and I know Nigel would never submit to your Matrix ... not that you've ever invited him."

"Should he wish to join as well, I certainly would not stand in his way. Yes, pleasures of the flesh can be a frustrating matter, but one can always find means around one's limitations. There are plenty of potential lovers within the Matrix."

"I am not leaving my husband."

"Very well. But do keep your beloved family in mind. Your continued resistance will only make things more difficult for them in the end."

"Are you threatening me?"

Carlina noticed Gaila quietly backing out into the main laboratory.

Fine, just leave me with him, she thought irritably. Though, really, she could hardly fault her friend. A quick retreat is the only reasonable defence against a vytoc.

"I am offering you immortality and great power," Mr. Géricault said. "Hardly a threat! That has been the dream of humankind for generations!"

"I like things the way they are."

"But you could have so much more."

"No."

"It would be unwise to try my patience."

"You know those sharp edges you mentioned?" Carlina said, looking the vytoc right in the eye. "I think that's all you are. You can sing? Well, so can a saw, but that doesn't stop it from being used to cut things apart. There is no beauty in you or your kind, Mr. Géricault. Now leave me alone."

"As you wish, then. Good-bye, my dear."

"Good-bye, Mr. Géricault."

He turned and began walking toward the entrance to the main laboratory, with Carlina following just a few paces behind him. Once she was at the doorway, however, the Facilitator spun around and lunged at her. Too late, she noticed the hypo-gun. It hit her before she had time to scream.

A sharp cold and the prickly sensation of pins and needles shot through her body. Icy daggers cut into her brain, forcing her muscles to contort. Her legs jerked out from under her as she fell, writhing, to the floor.

"At this point, of course, you have two avenues to choose from," Mr. Géricault said, softly. "You may consider mine the long term option. Au revoir, Carlina."

She did not hear him leave. In fact, she couldn't hear much of anything. But somewhere in the distance, someone was sobbing. It took a moment to realize it was her.

"Dr. White! Dr. White!"

"Are you all right, Doctor?"

"Carlina, are you there? Answer me!"

"Is this the afterlife," she moaned.

"No, you're still alive," Gaila reassured her. "He only gave you an addicting dose."

"Making things difficult."

"Not as difficult as he thinks," Gaila smiled. "Unlike most new addicts, you already have a support structure to fall back on."

"I do, don't I!" Carlina returned the smile as she rubbed the feeling back into her limbs.

"An' it's not like you're gonna lose all your friends, 'cause *we're* you're friends!" Serena chirped.

"And, if it's any consolation," Gaila added, helping Carlina to her feet. "You won't have to worry about using the protective gear from now on."

Looking around at the lab, at the star-fish tank, and the two ghost children, Carlina was hit by the true absurdity of her situation. The fact that he would do this *here* and think he was doing her harm was simply ludicrous.

"Doesn't think things through, does he?"

Chapter Ten

Another Monday morning had dawned – or at least, that's what the alarm clock said. Such matters as "day" and "night" become rather meaningless when you live in a windowless apartment tucked deep inside a massive skyscraper. Phil fumbled for the reset button and stumbled his way to the bathroom. Another day, another go-around of the same old routine: shower, shave, and dress. Then off to the kitchen to curse the general lack of coffee in Titan City.

In Phil's somewhat slanted memory, a proper day began with the aroma of coffee percolating; perhaps accompanied by the smell of bacon or sausage frying. There was little reason to get up otherwise. And a Monday would find Lara in the kitchen as well, making pancakes in the belief that they gave a sweet start to the work week.

But Lara wasn't in the kitchen, and the price of flour far too high to justify his trying to make such delicacies on his own. He could also forget about the simpler pleasures of a bowl of Corn Flakes or Raisin Bran. Cold cereal was just as impossible to buy as coffee, and even a simple loaf of toastable bread would set you back more than 30 sestri.

There was no sense in even *asking* about lingonberries.

Thus, breakfast had become a cruel and constant reminder of what he'd left behind: no wife, no coffee, no pancakes with lingonberries. And he'd never been able to stomach the meschelmash gruel that was the traditional Titanian start to the day. Instead, a couple fried eggs, a link of Latebran goat sausage, and a glass of tangerine juice would have to see him through to lunch. As for his caffeine fix, the only option available was bluethorn tea, made from the leaves of a badlands shrub.

According to Nigel, calling the substance "tea" was a sadistic joke and there was certainly no disagreeing with that. The stuff tasted more like spiced tree bark than tea.

"Merrow?" Something dark grey and furry rubbed against his lower legs.

"Awright. Here ya go, Seldon." Phil sliced off a sausage end and handed it down to the cat.

Hairy Seldon had been one of his rare concessions to domestic permanence, though, like most cat owners, he hadn't actually intended on getting one. Except that one day he'd found a kitten curled up on the seat of his motorcycle. It looked hungry. He fed it. And it hadn't left the apartment since.

"Well, fuzzface, it's off to another day at the salt mines," he said, giving the animal a scritch behind the ears before collecting his work satchel and heading out. "I promise I'll pick up some fishy* on the way home."

"Maow."

Phil lived in Tower 5, which put him fairly close to the

---

*   What Latebrans call "fishy" looks more like a large salamander than a terrestrial fish. Though the flesh can be eaten by humans, the taste is an acquired one at best. It's more commonly sold as cat food.

hospital tower, if not the actual hospital. Being that he was all the way down on level 63, the only difficulty he faced in getting to work, was waiting for what he liked to call his "L-evator"-- the large public vertical located next to Tower 9. Even at this hour, the thing took forever to come down.

He rode the lift only as far as level 75, getting off in the heart of the University district. In this part of town, the tea stands remained open around the clock, as their preferred clientèle could be counted on to keep odd hours.

Though it wasn't just a matter of keeping sleepy students awake. Bluethorn tea had a reputation for being an effective hangover remedy as well, and every pub in the district could boast at least one neighbouring tea stand.

And from the looks of things, sales should be good this morning. Phil found a crushed sandwich in the elevator (a waste of food no sober Titanian would allow) and a splattering of vomit greeted him as he stepped out onto the flat. Passing one of the larger pubs, he noticed the windows had been covered over with mesh screens. A closer inspection revealed several large holes in the glass.

"What happened over at Cubrick's?" He asked the tea-brewer.

"The usual muck and tussle," the man said, pouring the tea. "Couple of University boys with a bit too much spirit in 'em – you know how it is. Start off with a simple disagreement; get into a shouting match. Then, before you know it, the chairs start flyin'. 'Cept this time, one of 'em had a gun ... guess the green beans missed it during their raid last week."

"Anybody hurt?"

"Nah. Kid was so soused, it's a wonder he could hit the window. ... That'll be one sestrus, please."

"It's like my Old Man used to say, 'youth and stupidity go hand in hand!'" Phil tossed a few coins on the counter. "Keep the change."

Fortified by his cup of ersatz, Phil meandered his way down to the Tower 9 service docks, where Laas was loading up for the morning's run into Tylerville.

"Ready for another day at the races?"

"As ever," Phil said, taking another swig of the wretched drink. "Door's unlocked?"

"Yeah."

He opened up the cab and tried to make himself comfortable, while Laas made a few last minute checks with the loading crew.

"Hoy! Doctor Nielsen!" A familiar voice called out from the direction of the distribution centre.

"Wha?" Phil stuck his head out of the open door. "Oh...Hello, Mr. Doering. What's up?"

Saylor Doering sauntered over to the van.

"Bit of a change in plans, I'm afraid," he said cheerfully. "Seems our hobbyist won't be needing those parts for another year or so."

"You're calling off the run?" Phil asked in a low voice. "I thought we were ready to move."

"We were, but something came up."

"You don't mean the dormitory raid, do you?"

Saylor gave him a resigned look, his hands outstretched.

"Ah, yes... the raid," he sighed. "You know how it is when things don't quite go as planned. We put the guns in Laurence's room and somehow the beans start thinking it was Silas' dorm instead."

"Cat's on your tail, now, isn't he."

"For the moment, no," Saylor said, his grin fading. "The problem lies in Tylerville, I'm afraid. The effectiveness of our ammunition has come into question, and it's thrown our schedule off by ten months at the very least."

This explanation struck Phil as being a bit thin. *Like hell the Cat isn't on your ass,* he though, wondering what had really possessed Doering to come down here at this obscene hour, to tell him something he could have easily learned in Tylerville. There had to be something else going on. He thought back to the pub with the shot-out windows ... and University kids with guns.

The green beans might have missed one.

"By the way," he asked, matter of factly. "Silas wasn't mixed up with that business over at Cubricks, was he?"

"We know nothing about that," Saylor answered, a little too firmly. "And neither do you. Now be sure this message gets to Antony. Everything's on standby for at least ten months, maybe more. Understood?" He handed Phil a large, plain envelope secured with a wax seal.

"Yeah, I got it," Phil said, taking the envelope. "Just be sure to let me know when you want me to make another run."

He waved Doering good-bye and put the envelope in his work satchel, giving the wax seal a curious glance. Gummed envelopes were readily available in Titan City. So who was still using wax? The latest business fad, no doubt.

"What the hell was *that* about?" Laas asked, sliding into the driver's saddle.

"I think his kid's been grounded for a year."

"So... no more motorcycle parts?"

"Not for a year, anyway."

"In that case, if I were you, I'd pack up the Voorhees and get my arse to Tylerville. You'll want to be well away from that rat when the Cat starts closing in."

"Yeah, I'll leave eventually ... in a couple years, maybe."

"I mean now," Laas said, shifting the van into gear. "Take the chance while you still have it ... and you've got the fat bastard looking the other way!"

"Why? What do ya think *he's* gonna do? Put a hit on me, or something? C'mon! I'm the only reason the Resistance knows which end of the gun points where!"

"Teaching psychopaths to shoot firearms isn't the recipe for a long life," countered Laas. "I heard about what happened at Cubrick's. According to Mytchels, Silas was accusing one of your interns of being a tocker-lover – because he works for Newcomers, that is … *you!* When the kid tried to argue otherwise, Silas pulled the gun on 'im.

"Sorry, Phil, but that's who you're playing with and it's not Vyn Tyler. The Resistance is never going to see you as one of their own, and frankly … they scare the shit out of me."

"Laas, you're overreacting. They're being trained to shoot tockers, not people."

"Except people are easier to shoot. Plus, it's a firm bet Saylor Doering ain't operating with the best interests of the city in mind. Trust me on this, all right? Get out while you still can."

Chapter Eleven

"Right, Darling! Come to Daddy, now! Come on, Darling!"

Darling, meanwhile, was having none of it. Giving her father a reproachful stare, Sophia kept her grip firm on the edge of the sofa table.

"Come on! Take a step! You can do it!"

Slowly, one hand lifted from the table. Then the other. She was standing on her own, now. A little wobbly, perhaps, but standing. She looked around, as if wondering what to do next.

"Beautiful, Darling! Now, come on! Come to Daddy! There's a good girl!"

Darling's response was to fall flat on her bottom.

"Bahp!"

"I think," Robyn said, dangling from one end of the sofa. "She don't wanna walk."

Nigel was beginning to agree. Sophia was in no rush to take those vaunted first steps. Instead, she crawled over to where Kitti lay and began pushing it around, content to remain on her hands and knees.

"Tha's mine!"

"Come now. You can share."

"No!"

In one acrobatic move, Robyn was off the sofa, and wrenching the fluffy pull-toy from his sister's arms.

"Mine!"

"Muaaaaaa!"

Nigel fought back the words immediately coming to mind as he stepped into the fray.

"I'll have that, thank you," he said, taking the toy.

"Mine!"

"Not any more, young man."

Praying their mother would get home before he throttled one or both of them, he set Kitti on top of the tallest bookcase and planted Robyn in the "think about it" chair.

"You've got five minutes. Remember, you wouldn't be here if you had shared your things."

"Kitti's mine!"

The boy kicked at the wall, but he knew better than to get up.

"Want Mama!"

"Mummy will be home shortly, but I grant you, she won't be giving any reprieves."

He returned to the living room to find that Sophia had turned her attention to Robyn's latest block castle. A sizable portion had already been knocked down and she was happily building a new edifice from the rubble.

"Getting even are you?"

"Gah!"

But at least it was quiet again.

Saturday afternoons had always been Carlina's "day

off," when she could have a little time to herself. She'd be off visiting her mother, getting her hair done, or working out at the fitness centre, leaving Nigel to take care of the children. Generally, this wasn't a difficult assignment, as the children spent much of the time napping while he watched the soccer matches.

> *And that ends our halftime report. For those of you just clicking in, this is Jym Voss, the voice of Titan City, with Karl Wylson in the newly renovated Soc-11 Soccer Centre, level 200.*
> *And it's been an amazing first half, with the Sparks of the Electricians Guild putting up a strong fight against the Domecocks of the Dome Maintenance Union. Score at the half is 4 to 3 in favour of the Domecocks.*
> *The boys are coming out on the weave now. First kick is going to be between Lundon and Matryk.*

To be strictly technical, Titanian soccer was nothing more than football played indoors. But Nigel could never bring himself to call it "football."

True football was played on grass, on the actual ground. *Not* in a carpeted stadium on top of a 200 story skyscraper. And you had to be out in the weather – it was essential, weather. Especially the brutal weather that turned the pitch into a mud bath and made sitting through the full ninety-plus minutes an act of heroism.

One good rainstorm – or better yet, snow – and you knew who the *real* fans were!

Nevertheless, there was one aspect of the Titanian game that he enjoyed immensely, and that was the fact that sports here did not conform to any particular season. He'd happily discovered that he could watch a soccer match very nearly every Saturday afternoon. Come to think of it, that might have something to do with why Carlina chose Saturdays as her "day off."

> *Looks like Patryks is closing in on goal, but he's got Lem and Terri hot on his heels! He passes to Matryk! And it's.........Augh! Excellent save from the Domecock's goaltender.*

Four months had passed since the attack on Carlina and while things had certainly changed, they hadn't changed *that much*. After all, vytasynene addiction was only noticeable if you were born that way.

Or asked an addict an uncomfortable question. It was the truth serum aspect of the drug that made social outcasts of those it addicted. To be sure, the Whites *had* seen a noticeable drop in invitations over the holidays, but their core circle of friends remained unchanged.

No doubt, Mr. Géricault had thought to hurt them financially with his little trick and, admittedly, the hospital was less than excited to have a second vytasynene addict working in their pharmacy. Carlina had been demoted back to part-time assistant, but she still kept her Thursday night "special work" as well as the stipend that came with it. That was only fair, as she was now better qualified to handle vytasynene than she had been before.

Food was an issue, but for Titanians, it always is. Nigel's Newcomer benefits had run out the previous year and both children were too old now to qualify for the "baby allotments" given to new mothers. That left their corporate rations, which had naturally taken a hit with Carlina's demotion.

Ready money was an option, up until you saw the prices.

Still, they were getting by, largely on account of Carlina's green thumb. The overgrowth in the dining room had increased considerably, with more and more vegetables added to the greenery. Meanwhile, Phil continued to give them his ration cards and even Gaila had chipped in as well, bringing over milk and eggs and even the occasional chicken. Evidently, the ghost children had quite the colony hidden away in the city's lowest levels, complete with a sizeable hydro, chicken house, and a small herd of goats.

Carlina benefited the most, of course, by having a Newcomer husband. A native Titanian would have left her at the start and taken the children with him. Whereas Nigel, on the other hand, was determined to stay and keep the family together, no matter what the difficulties. In many ways, their marriage was stronger now than ever.

Add that to the list of Mr. Géricault's miscalculations. Those vytoc enhancements he was always on about must not affect the brain.

And that went waaaaaay over! A missed
opportunity by Lundon.
   Lem has the ball now...but not for long! Matryk
has the intercept, but Lundon takes it from him!
   And...off the ceiling to Patryks! It's anybody's
game now!
   Lem has it again!

"Five minutes up?" A voice squeaked from the hallway.

"Yes. You can go ahead and play. But you have to share."

"'Kay."

Robyn sat down on the other side of the block pile, opposite Sophia, and for one brief, shining moment, the two children played quietly together. Only too late did Nigel realize he should have taken a picture.

   Another great catch by Lynsey for the Sparks!
   Coach Voights is calling for a substitution. Ronni Lem
is coming off the field to be replaced by...is it? Yes! Zack
Maartyns coming in at the 73rd minute for the Domecocks!
   Number 13, Maartyns is a five time winner of the Butter
Boot and has helped bring the Domecocks to the Intercity
Championships three times...

"Hey! Dos'r my blocks!"

"Robyn!" Nigel warned.

"Awright, here. Des'r yours an' des'r mine, 'kay?"

"Pah!"

   Lynsey gives the ball to Matryk and he's running in
the clear. But Maartyns is right on his heels! What a fight!
Ow! That had to be a foul.
   Sure looked like it. But the referees are checking the replay.
   Maartyns isn't waiting around! He's going for the goal...
hold it! Matryk is right on top of him!

He wants that penalty kick!

"Giv'it back! Tha wasn't in yor pile!"

"Gaaaah!"

"Mine!"

"Meeeaaah!"

"'Kay. You can *hav*'it den!"

They're really fighting for it! No, I mean really!
And now Terri and Patryks are joining in.
It's a regular brawl out there!

"No! Tha' was mine!"

"Gaaah!"

"Don' throw tha at me! I'll throw it at you!"

"Darling! I'm home, and … JUST WHAT IS GOING ON AROUND HERE!"

Here comes the referee Jym, and he does not look happy.

"She started it!"

"Maaa!"

"Get to your room! Right now!"

"No!"

"NOW!"

Ooh! Red cards all around!

Nigel's ears had barely registered his wife's return before she disappeared into the nursery. By the time he was able to give her a decent "hello," Robyn was back to staring at the wall and Sophia had been deposited in her crib.

Carlina collapsed wearily onto the sofa.

"Guess I won't ask how your day went," she said, looking up at Kitti perched on the bookcase. A bit of puffiness around her eyes told him that she'd been crying recently, and it wasn't because of the children.

He switched off the game.

"What happened?"

"I'm out of the fitness centre for one," she said, holding up the wrist on which she wore her dosage timer. "Old Mrs. Lanner recognized the timer and started wagging her tongue around. Of course, when the manager asked, I couldn't lie to her...and that was that."

"Don't the ghost children have a health centre now? They have everything else."

"They do, but that's a long way down," she sighed. "Besides, that's not the worst of it."

"There's worse?"

Carlina nodded.

"Been feeling a little odd recently, so I went over to Kathi's today."

"What's wrong?"

She had his full attention now. Kathi was Dr. Arlen, Carlina's physician.

"It seems vytasynene can neutralize certain forms of birth-control," she said, giving him a wan smile. "Looks like I'm pregnant again."

Chapter Twelve

Like most deserts, the badlands of Latebra know only two seasons, wet and dry, and even vytoc would agree the wet season is the preferable one. Such is the winter, when the days are tolerably warm and the rainwater running down the sides of the dome help to augment the city's water supply. But winters are brief and gradually, the rain must give way to the blazing sun of summer.

Now it was July, and the city was awakening to another day of high heat and oppressive humidity. From the tallest towers, solar sails unfurled, demanding that the sun compensate, at least a little, for the increased energy needed to keep things comfortable.

Far out in the badlands, where Titan was nothing more than a gleam on the horizon, the unnamed road stretched through a rocky outcropping, coming to an end at the back of a box canyon. Here lay a macabre garden of rusted and weathered wreckage; the remains of ships beached light years from the oceans they once sailed. Divested of crews, cargo, and anything else that might appear useful, the hulks had been left to the desert – testament to lives altered forever by vytoc whim.

In the midst of these derelicts, the air seemed to waver, and it wasn't merely an effect of the heat. The very fabric of space rippled and folded, finally pulling back to disgorge a dark, sleek shape onto the anonymous road.

To be sure, a black, Firebird hardtop probably wasn't the best choice of vehicle in which to be driving down a desert highway in the middle of summer. But the promise of an open road with neither traffic nor speed limit was something Natonoc could never pass up.

He was keeping a wary eye on the temperature gauge, however. Immune though he was to the poisons in the planet's atmosphere, it was still a long walk should the engine give out. As a precaution, he'd loaded the boot (or "trunk" rather; it was an American car) with extra supplies of water and petrol, and he had timed the portal to give himself an early morning start. Still, the air was already steaming hot, in prelude to the scorcher to come. But the engine, while running warmer than he'd like, didn't appear to be overheating ... yet. With luck, they would make it into Titan before it turned critical.

"Interesting old house, but it looks only half there," Talonyvoc was saying from the passenger seat, thumbing through an envelope full of photographs. "I'm assuming some remodelling has been done?"

"You could say that," said Natonoc. "The original house was built in 1691 as a small hunting lodge and, as these things go, didn't remain a small hunting lodge for very long. You should have seen it when my uncle first acquired it! They even tried to recreate the 'hall of mirrors' from Versailles. I am positive that if there is a Hell, it will be done over in Rococo.

"Thankfully, most of the worst burned down in '89.

About all that was left was the central staircase and the north wing of the Old Manor. What you see there is the result of my uncle's attempts at restoration."

"Baroque-Victorian with a few modern accents thrown in. I can see where you just *had* to have it."

"Call me sentimental, but this does keep it in the family. Had to fight off some idiot developer as it was. Friend of Randolph's, and God knows what he wanted it for! Would have torn it down most likely. My cousins and their children haven't been the best stewards and Randolph's the worst by far. He hasn't had the land ten years and, in that time, has sold off almost the whole estate. The bridal path boasts a row of shops now, and the rest of the land's gone to housing of a most vulgar design. The house, itself, is left to one minuscule acre – a swan among ducklings!"

"I wouldn't use the word 'swan,' exactly."

"Goose then. I'm hoping to turn it into a way house. It's a nice, central location. A good addition, I think, to Inverness and Colchester."

"I suppose, but...Manchester?"

"Can't be helped, that. My uncle was quite the man in Manchester, not to mention Liverpool, and just about every other port of call in the British Empire. Made his money in shipping and later -- sad to say -- war profiteering. He was one of the few men in England still on his feet in '46. Pity he died that year."

"It will be interesting to hear what the Council decides. I'm assuming the current owners have no idea who their buyer is."

"That's the beauty of solicitors, my friend!" Natonoc grinned, his eyes turning a cheerful yellow. "Everything goes through my man, Wentworth, and Randolph only knows me by the name on the bid. At no time does he ever get close enough to notice that his Mr. Archer looks almost exactly like his father's black-sheep cousin."

"Who knows," Talonyvoc said, putting the envelope with the pictures back in the glove box. "You might get me to England yet, one of these days."

He stretched an arm out the open window, letting the air slip past his fingers.

"Are we there yet," he yawned.

"Should be getting close," Natonoc replied, still keeping a concerned orange eye on his temperature gauge. "And unless that's a mirage, I see the gate ahead."

A small pulse of energy from Natonoc's linking crystal brought the barricade to life. It moved aside and minutes later, they were merging onto the Commercial Route, heading for Titan City.

"Glasses time, boys. Coriolon! You awake?"

"Whu?"

"The Boss says to put on your glasses," Talonyvoc said as a figure unfolded itself from the narrow confines of the

Firebird's rear seat.

Coriolon rubbed at his glowing blue eyes as he sat up.

"S'where are we?"

"The Emerald City," Natonoc deadpanned, as Titan's towers loomed before them.

"Really? Wonder what I should ask the Wizard for?"

"Better glasses, perhaps?"

They had no issues with the customs agents as they passed through the city's gateway and certainly no inspection. It wasn't because of the dark glasses. Any vehicle travelling with open windows outside the dome was allowed through, no questions asked.

Now for the tricky part.

Natonoc hated driving in Titan City, not because it was complicated, but because it was so slow. Thanks to the narrow, tightly twisting nature of the city's rampways, traffic seldom moved faster than 20mph and on the Periphery, the speed limit was 40.

Ignoring the limit, the Firebird raced up the Periphery at 60mph, taking advantage of the light traffic on the lower levels. Turning inward at level 45, Natonoc slowed it down to 30mph, as he climbed to the fiftieth level and the service lane that led into the Black Tower's car park.

He parked next to the two Land Rovers, in a place marked with the dancing red devil of Manchester United.

"At least nobody's taken our spot," Coriolon said,

brightly.

"They remember what happened last time."

Getting out of the car, Natonoc gave it a quick once-over. No dents or dings, but the sides were streaked reddish-grey from the dust.

"Wonder if there is a car wash nearby."

"I know of some van wash places on level 30," suggested Talonyvoc. "They should have a stall big enough to fit this beast."

"And there's always the fire hose if they don't," added Coriolon.

But that was neither here nor there. Natonoc unlatched the trunk and pulled out three long coats, causing a sudden shift in conversation.

"You don't really expect us to wear those, do you?"

"Regulations, sailor. Star devils wear dark glasses and long, dark coats."

"Can't we switch to light jackets in the summertime?"

"You'd never look intimidating in a jacket."

"But I don't want to look intimidating," Coriolon whined. "I want to look like the fun guy people invite to parties and buy drinks for!"

"Just put on the coat, Cor."

Now suitably overdressed, the three of them sauntered along, into the lifts and out onto the ninetieth level. Human employees -- secretaries and Security Service agents alike -- gave them a wide berth as they passed.

Indeed, they made for an unusual procession: Natonoc was in the lead; 6'7" and gratuitously thin. He had long, reddish-orange hair, which contrasted nicely with his deep purple, Victorian-style morning coat.

Next came Coriolon, a foot shorter, with a round, boyish face, and black hair cut in the Mod style. In deference to his past vocation, he wore a coat of navy blue, with white cording and shiny brass buttons.

Bringing up the rear was Talonyvoc, almost as tall as Natonoc but not as gaunt. He had fine, medium-length brown hair that generally looked windblown even when he *hadn't* been riding in a car with the windows open. His coat was a black canvas duster with lots of pockets.

Between them, they carried a minimum of two handguns apiece, plus a cutlass, a dagger, and five switchblades.

"We'll need to stop at the canteen," Talonyvoc mentioned, as they passed a commissary designated for humans only. "I have a delivery to make."

"I thought Tapioca Terrorism was done for," Natonoc said, pointing a thumb at Coriolon.

"Seems not everyone was terrorized, " replied Talonyvoc, taking a small box from his pocket. It bore a handwritten label, which read: CAT FOOD.

As for the Cat in question, they found him alone in his

office, aimlessly bouncing a small rubber stress ball off the walls and filing cabinets.

"About *time* you showed up!"

"We would have been here sooner, but Tonners took a wrong turn at Albuquerque."

"Happens all the time," confessed Natonoc.

"In other words, you brought the car," Kittyvoc sighed.

"I prefer to call it 'taking the scenic route.'"

"And I would prefer that you use the local from now on. But as you're here, let's get started."

He reached into a drawer and pulled out several chunks of what looked like thick glass.

"You know what these are, I presume?"

"Cultured quartz," Talonyvoc replied. "That appears to have been hit quite forcefully."

"Shot, actually," said Kittyvoc. "It seems our old dogs of the Resistance have taught themselves a new trick."

"What? Shooting quartz?"

"Shooting thick crystal," he explained. "Gooch got these from Detective Vantuinen out in Tylerville, who tripped over them during an investigation of his own. Said he was worried this meant the Vyn people were working on something a bit bigger than pistols.

"So, remembering our little sortie up at the University a couple years back, I had Foz drop in on our gate inspectors for a few random inspections of his own. Liaison Office made him stop, but not before he caught the gun runner."

He opened a dossier, pulling out several forms covered in Portysanon's precise handwriting. Attached was a photograph framed in bright orange.

"Our courier was a Dr. Philippe Toussant Nielsen, an oncologist brought here in '63 and a fixture on the watch list practically from the start. Tried to round one on Portysanon the very day he arrived and put himself in hospital trying to escape shortly thereafter."

"I trust you have him in holding now," said Natonoc.

"Not for a minute!" Kittyvoc exclaimed. "If anything, the man has my sympathy. Considering he was forced, quite unexpectedly, to leave wife and family to come here, I can't honestly blame him for wanting to even the score a little. No, Foz let him go -- though not before putting a tracer in with his contraband."

He tossed several long, narrow bullet casings onto the desktop.

"Naturally, they had warning once the raid came, but we did find a few more quartz targets and plenty of brass. The weapon appears to be some kind of rifle, though I doubt it's much bigger than a sten gun. With the mayoral elections coming up, it's imperative that we find this weapon or weapons before someone does something stupid with them.

"One word of warning, however. While I doubt the

gun can hurt us too much, the bullets *are* designed to shatter silicon-based matrices. Don't get too reckless."

"My dear Cat," Natonoc boasted. "We are the epitome of safe and sober duty."

"Ha!" Kittyvoc shot back, bouncing the stress ball off Natonoc's chest.

"Now, we'll need to keep this as quiet as possible," he continued, using a key to lock both the bullet casings and the dossier in a desk drawer. "Liaison Office is mixed in with this somehow, so you'll have to get information to me through a third party."

"Gooch?" Talonyvoc asked.

"Who else? I've already sent word around that you're here to help him with another murder probe."

"More dead ghost children?"

"Dead Council member," Kittyvoc said, getting serious again. "Anyone want to take a guess on which one?"

"David Cawthorn?"

"Kewpie doll for Talonyvoc!"

"I suppose Daniel is the prime suspect again," Natonoc said, with more than a hint of sarcasm in his tone. "He's a hit man now? Bringing down his own uncle?"

"I suspect it's another attempt to flush him out," Kittyvoc replied, returning the quartz to its proper cabinet. This too was secured with a mechanical lock.

"Naturally, nobody would admit to seeing him at the

funeral," he said. "His uncle was shot twice in the Civic Tower parking zone, and so far we're at a loss for decent witnesses. The chauffeur says he only heard the shot, though another driver in the area mentioned seeing a dark figure fleeing the scene. So far, we've talked to six people, and can't get a good description from any one of them.

"There's been speculation that Doering's behind this, though I'm not entirely convinced. While he's no friend of Cawthorn's, he's usually a bit more subtle than this."

"Think it might be the same person who killed Cassandra Manning?" Suggested Coriolon, pulling down his glasses to reveal eyes glowing reddish-orange.

Kittyvoc gave him a thin half-smile.

"Just find me some answers," he told them. "Communicate, like I said, through Detective Gooch, although it's possible you might catch Fosteperon a time or two having lunch at Lovell's Soup Shop. Just stay clear of me and headquarters unless I – and only I -- tell you otherwise."

"Who are you again?"

"Get out of here!"

"They still haven't caught Danny, then?" Coriolon asked Talonyvoc, as they made their way up to the main entrance.

"Despite a close call a couple years ago," Talonyvoc said. "I believe he's still safe with his mother."

"Still living with the ghost children?"

"Ja. Sadly, it was his half-brother who took the bullet. We were helping to improve their defences when I was sent home last."

"That seems to be the procedure around here," Coriolon grumbled. "We come in to find something amiss, and just when we're about to get it all worked out, they tell us to go home again."

The others nodded in assent.

Wordlessly, they made their way down the hall, each lost in his own thoughts.

"Ah, gentlemen! A moment please?"

Three pairs of dark glasses turned in unison as Gerysalon stepped out from a side office.

"Cat told me he was bringing in linewalkers to help with the Cawthorn probe," he said, with unusual affability.

"That appears to be the case."

"Did he tell you about the hospital yet?"

"What happened at the hospital?" Talonyvoc asked.

"Well," Gerysalon gave them a conspiratorial look. "There has been some question as to the extent of the Councilman's original injuries. In fact, it's interesting that his condition was actually pronounced as stable only hours before he died."

"You think it was a *doctor* who murdered him?"

"Cat's known for some time about Resistance activity at Research Hospital, which was where Councilman Cawthorn was treated. And though he was never charged, one researcher in particular matches the description of a suspect in a shooting against the Prefect some time ago."

Talonyvoc lowered one side of his glasses so that Natonoc could see the reddish glow of his eyes. Natonoc nodded.

"Very interesting," he lied to Gerysalon. "Have you any other information?"

Chapter Thirteen

"Security Services! Surprise inspection!"

"Aw, fer...don't you guys ever knock!"

"He did say it was a surprise."

Phil snapped his head around as the star-devils entered the lab. For a moment, he thought he heard the Australian coming in. But his ears were telling him no, the accent was too refined; more like Nigel's.

"We apologize for the inconvenience," continued the redheaded star-devil, the one who sounded British. "But we need to scan your files and check the access networks on the computers. It will only take a minute."

"Doubt they'll make much sense to you," said Nigel, who was giving the redhead a look of absolute hatred, mixed with curiosity.

"Not to worry. We brought a doctor."

Phil recognized one of the other star-devils as being the German who gave him the pudding. Unfortunately, Dr. Trug also seemed to recognized him.

"I thought you would have moved to Tylerville by now," he said, conversationally, coming over to Phil's work station.

"Well, you know ... I was planning to. And then something came up, and then we started having some success with the new chemo, and...so..."

"Being caught with contraband is usually enough to revoke one's travel permit."

"Pending a review," Phil said, defensively. "And I've got a good lawyer. It'll all wash over in a month or two."

But Dr. Trug wasn't really listening. Instead, his attention was on Phil's computer. He was running through the files at an incredible speed and without the need for a compustylus. Somehow, the star-devil could get the machine to do whatever he wished just by staring at it head-on.

"That crystal helps you read the files, doesn't it?"

"It's quite handy that way," acknowledged the star-devil. "I see you've been working with vytasynene."

"Yeah. Just a side project, though," Phil told him. "Been trying to duplicate the regenerative effects. So far, I've found a few promising ways to repair nerve damage, but only in ghost children. Guess I got a ways to go before I figure out the whole process."

"You have your work cut out for you, Doctor. As you know, vytasynene alters the genetic code of the victim. An unaffected patient will not respond in the same way as a ghost child."

"Which brings up something I noticed awhile back," Phil said. "I once had a ghost child sitting here when a Facilitator walked in. It was like she could sense his presence in the hall before he even got to the door."

"They do feel a resonance," Dr. Trug confirmed. "As

the drug is very close in composition to vytoc neural fluids. Some have made the case that those born with the addiction should be considered partially joined, and therefore constitute a form of proto-vytoc."

"What did you say?" Nigel's ears had picked up on their conversation and he was hurriedly crossing over to them.

"His wife was given an addicting dose a couple years ago," Phil explained.

"Attacked in her own laboratory by your Chief Liaison Officer," Nigel added. "And now you're telling me my son is a proto-vytoc?"

Despite his eyes being completely covered, Dr. Trug's stare was penetrating.

"You name wouldn't happen to be 'White,' would it?"

"It would, yes. Nigel White. You may remember my wife from an incident involving her sister, Christina Manning."

"When did the assault happen?" Dr. Trug asked, shaking Nigel's hand.

"Day after Christina was released."

The star-devil nodded. Immediately, Phil's computer returned to its main menu screen, and Dr. Trug turned toward his red-headed companion, currently seated at Nigel's computer.

"You have the primary, Nat. Find anything?"

"Only some schematics for an old-style Kalashnikov,"

he replied. "Nothing incriminating."

"Kalashnikov?!"

Nigel about crossed the lab in one step. On his computer screen was a detailed diagram for an automatic rifle.

"I never!"

"We know," Dr. Trug assured him. "Obviously, the program was planted, though I suspect it was originally meant for someone other than us to find."

"All it would take is another assassination attempt," the redhead said, thoughtfully. "And a word to the Security Services..."

"Und while our Doctor White may not have the *actual* weapon, there will be evidence that he could make it if he wanted to."

"And he's a Bolshevik as well, the cad!" The redhead gave them a sideways grin as he deleted the program.

"Again, we apologize for the intrusion," Dr. Trug said to the lab in general as he and the other star-devil took their leave.

"Come along, Cor!"

"What? So soon?" The third star-devil stuck his head out of Dr. Spaulding's office. He was very nearly talking to himself.

"Hey! Wait for me!"

Catching the door before it could latch, Phil put his ear to the crack, listening as the star-devils talked in the hall.

"Now *that* was enlightening," he heard Dr. Trug saying.

"You think Ger's in on this somehow?"

"Up to his neck!"

"So, what's next?"

"We go hunting."

"Splendid! What's the quarry?"

"Québecois."

"Isn't that a soup?"

"More like a stew once we've caught up with him."

Then they must have turned a corner because he could no longer make out the words. Finally, he allowed the door to latch.

"So, wadaya know! Turns out the Frog's a Canuck!"

"What's a who?" Asked an intern.

"That Facilitator, Géricault. He's a Canadian! And here all this time I thought he was French."

"Does it matter?" The intern clearly wasn't following any of this.

"Good point," Phil said, returning to his work station. "They're SOB's no matter what country they're from."

Out of the corner of his eye, he noticed Dr. Swendon going into the incubator room. Moving casually, as though he wasn't *actually* following, he followed the other man inside, closing the door behind him.

Lionel had been recently promoted, taking over Dr.

Spaulding's position in the wake of Dr. Peris' retirement. Phil had been one of those recommending him – a decision he was beginning to regret.

"Okay, buddy, out with it," he said into the younger man's ear. "Who put that shit on Nage's computer?"

"What? You can't figure it out?"

"Look you!" He grabbed Lionel by the lapels. "If this is some joke of Doering's, I ain't laughing. Okay?"

"Come off it, Phil. It was your own little tocker buddies, all right!"

"What tocker buddies? You know I'm no friend of theirs."

"So you say," Lionel sneered. "You seemed to be damned friendly just a little bit ago. And I know for a fact it was a star devil that done it."

"You jackin' me around?"

"Not at all." Lionel seemed to be enjoying Phil's dismay. "It was yesterday at lunch. Some tocker in dark glasses comes in and says he needs to use a computer. Didn't know what he was doing, but I guess we do now, eh?"

He gave Phil a cruel grin.

"And is it really just a coincidence that the green beans raided our training area just a day after you got caught at the gate?"

"Okay, so they followed me," Phil said, silently cursing himself for the lapse. "But that don't make me a collaborator."

"That'd better be true," Lionel whispered. "Because the kettle's about to boil. And trust me, you bust us on this one and there won't be enough left of you to fill a sample slide."

He walked out, leaving Phil standing alone and confused in the dimly lit room. Absolutely nothing the man said had made sense.

Did Dr. Trug *really* plant a weapon schematic on Nigel's computer? Or was there something else going on that Lionel wasn't telling him? And just how many of them considered him a collaborator? What about Doering? What about *Silas*?

Something Laas had once said scratched at the back of his memory. Obviously, he was going to have to do something to prove himself and, if Lionel's last threat was any indication, it looked as if an opportunity would be coming his way *very* soon.

Chapter Fourteen

It was a game called "Colour Wheel." Popular with college students, it consisted of six coloured panels set in a ring. The panels would light up in a particular sequence and the players would then have to copy the sequence in order to earn points.

There was also a children's version. It only had three colours.

Red. Blue. Red. Yellow. Blue. Red.

Nine-month-old Jonathan watched the flashing lights intently.

"Gah! Bah! Gah! Bee! Bah! Gah!" He squealed, smashing his pale fist down onto the panels. The machine responded with a brisk fanfare:

"YOU ARE COR-RECT!"

"Have you considered music lessons?" Dr. Myrna asked, switching the machine to the next level.

"He *has* shown an interest in the piano," Carlina confessed, as her youngest breezed through another sequence. "Though right now we try to keep him away from it. His playing has been referred to as the 'Anvil Chorus.'"

"Well, you've either got a musician on your hands or a genius for algorithms," Dr. Myrna said. "At his age, he should still be trying to figure out the first level. And this thing's set at three already and hasn't stumped him yet."

"YOU ARE COR-RECT!"

She switched off the game.

"Naaaaaaah!"

"Sorry, kid. Playtime's over." She reached for her clipboard. "So far, so good. Intelligence is clearly well above average. He's still underweight, but that's hardly unusual for his kind... heart and lungs look fine, but eyes remain a concern. Best keep an eye on 'em, so to speak, and keep him away from bright lights. Has he been sick at all recently?"

"A slight fever a couple weeks ago, but he seems to be over it."

"His dosage still two hours?"

"Yes. Gaila says it'll be another six months before we can begin lengthening the intervals."

"I see he's already walking."

"He's always had strong legs."

Carlina was smiling, but there was a shadow of concern in her eyes. She glanced over at Sophia, dozing in the ride-a-long.

Dr. Myrna caught the glance.

"She'll walk when she's good and ready."

"But she just turned three," Carlina whined. "She's getting too big for the ride-a-long!"

"You won't want to hear this, but with mongloidy, it can sometimes take up to five years. On the other hand, she does show a normal intelligence, it just so happens that her processor's a little slow."

As she spoke, Dr. Myrna was giving Jonathan his latest vaccination. The boy barely took notice of the needle, simply giving his paediatrician a curious look as she withdrew it from his leg.

"I need more patients like this," she said, half to herself. "I love a kid who isn't afraid of needles."

"He does find them irritating if they disturb his playtime."

"I can appreciate that. All right, kiddo," Dr. Myrna finished as Carlina wrestled Jonathan back into his shirt. "I officially pronounce you sound as the dome wall and I'll be seeing you again in three months for your first yearly."

"Bah! Bah-gah?"

"And we'll play more 'Colour Wheel,' I promise."

"Ga'aah!"

Carlina bid Dr. Myrna good-bye and slid Jonathan into the upper berth of the ride-a-long. It was currently set as a reclining baby seat, but that would have to be changed soon. The boy was very nearly pulling himself out, trying to get a better look at where they were going.

In the waiting area, they met up with Christina, who was busy entertaining Robyn at the activity table. They had built up a complex network of interconnecting plastic chutes, through which they were running a large marble.

"We really need to get a set of these."

"For Robyn or for you?"

"Get it for Robbie and I'll babysit more!"

"I'll think about it," Carlina said, rolling her eyes.

Pulling a reluctant Robyn from the activity table, she herded her small flock outside. The clinic was located on the 85th level flat, only two towers from home -- but why hurry?

"How's everybody for ice cream?"

"IdoIdoIdo!" Robyn squealed.

"That's one," Christina laughed. "We could always go up to Willyferd's"

"IdoIdoIdo!"

"Willyferd's it is, then."

Even though they were near the centre of the city, where little sunlight could reach, the air was still suffocatingly hot. Add the usual Titanian humidity, and even the short walk to the verticals felt like a long slog through gelatin. But there was some respite to be had in the cool rush of air as the vertical pushed upward. And, of course, the ice cream parlour would be air conditioned.

More to the point, they would be somewhere *other* than home.

The addition of Jonathan had turned the family's child care situation into a nightmare. None of the usual agencies, including the Titan Center for Special Needs, would admit a ghost child. And while the "colony" was an option, they were too far down-level to be very practical. Carlina had quit her day job to care for her son on her own, with the result that the family now had even *less* money to spend on child care. Robyn, at least, had progressed to the government-subsidised Middle City Kindergarten. But Sophia continued to go to the Center for Special Needs, and the tuition there wasn't getting any cheaper. As it was, she remained on a half-day schedule.

Christina helped when she could, but more and more of her time was being spent with the theatre. She was beginning to make quite a name for herself, reprising the role of Lynessa in a televised version of *Wider Horizons* and, most recently, landing the lead role in a City Rep production of *The Girl in Tower Seven*. If she kept *that* up, Carlina mused, she just might find herself supporting the rest of the family.

"Look, Sis! I'm on the marquee!"

The Titan Repertory Theater, along with Willyferd's ice cream parlour, was located on the 100th level, on a flat known as "The Bridges." This was Titan's arts district, home to three theatres, the symphony hall, and a wide assortment of boutiques and art galleries. It's public areas were populated by jugglers, puppeteers, and wandering musicians.

"Ba'ah!" Jonathan cried, reaching out to a man playing a twelve-string.

"No, Jonapet," Christina chided. "You don't want a guitar."

"Although Dr. Myrna did suggest music lessons."

"She obviously hasn't heard the Anvil Chorus, then,"

said Christina. "Though I guess he could play drums."

Upon entering Willyferd's, Christina found a table and got the children settled, while Carlina went up to the counter to place their order.

"Five small strawberry swirl, please."

"That will be eight sestri, seventy-five."

She ran her bank card through the reader, trying not to think about the fact that nine sestri could have bought a dozen eggs instead...or a box of meschel crispbread...or 300 grams of goat meat.

You can be practical tomorrow, she told herself, pushing the money worries aside.

Being that it was such a hot day, the place was fairly crowded, and the only table Christina could find was in the centre of the shop. Carlina could feel the stares all around as she fed her curiously pale son.

Just ignore them. There were no laws saying a ghost child couldn't go out in public – at least, not yet. So she tried to concentrate on the ice cream, while Christina chattered on about the latest rehearsal gossip and a guitar quartet serenaded outside.

"Yoo hoo, Jon! Over here … ice cream!"

Too soon, however, the ice cream was gone and it was time to clean up the children and head for home. But there was more than the usual matter of sticky faces to contend with, today. Sophia had managed to get a fair amount in her hair.

"Uh, Sis? This might've been a bad idea," Christina said, as Carlina worked to get the goo out of the little girl's braids.

"How so?"

"Let's just say this place is too damned popular."

That's when she heard the footsteps coming up behind her.

"Good afternoon, mademoiselle; madame."

Thanks in part to Christina's warning, Carlina didn't jump, but looked up calmly into the face of Mr. Géricault.

"Well, it was a good afternoon."

"Really, my dear? Is that any way to greet an old friend?"

"Bad man! Pow!" Robyn cried, pointing his forefinger, thumb raised, at the Facilitator. Admittedly, it was no less effective than any other gun used against a vytoc.

"Pow! Pow!"

"I think its time we went to the little people's room,"*Christina said, grabbing Robyn's arm and practically dragging him to the lavatories.

"They're a little high-spirited at that age," commented Carlina, stopping just short of an apology.

"I see the family has grown since the last time we

---

* "Little people's" rooms are common in Titan's public areas and in those establishments which cater to children. Fitted with changing tables and child-size facilities, they allow parents to take care of their young ones without having to go into the adult lavatories; therefore avoiding the embarrassment that so often arises when an adult must attend to a small child of the opposite sex.

met."

"Jonathan was born last October."

"They told me you had left the pharmacy. Must be difficult with three children to feed."

"We're managing."

Carlina finished re-braiding Sophia's hair and began loading her daughter back into the ride-a-long. As she turned around, she noticed the odd trio standing just inside the entrance.

Star-devils?

She recognized Mr. Trug from the day Christina was arrested, and wondered why he and his friends appeared to be shadowing Mr. Géricault. Bodyguard, perhaps?

"Your husband is up for promotion again. He won't get it, you know," Mr. Géricault was saying.

"Same as last year, then. We rather suspected you had a hand in that."

"And if he were dismissed entirely … what then?"

"Then he finds another position."

"Perhaps there is no other position."

"There's always Riverside," Carlina said, giving the Facilitator a defiant look. "He's geriatric qualified. They'd hire him in a minute."

"Are you sure about that? Charity hospitals are far from independent."

"Then we'll move to Tylerville."

"Without a travel pass? I think not."

"We'll find something," she said weakly, setting Jonathan into his berth. She was having trouble fastening the safety straps as her fingers kept fumbling with the buckles. Everyone in Willyferd's could hear what the Facilitator was saying to her, and everyone was staring, including people watching from outside. Her face was hot, flushed with humiliation.

"We'll live with the ghost children if we have to."

"Will you now?"

In a blur of motion, Mr. Géricault ripped the straps from the ride-a-long and pulled Jonathan out by his shirt. Before Carlina could process what was happening, the vytoc was headed outside, with her child dangling upside down from his hand. The whole world seemed to echo with screaming.

For a moment, she just stood there, frozen. *What is he doing? Where's he taking my baby?!* Finding her legs at last, she began running after him.

But what can I do? He's a Facilitator!

Dr. Trug?

But the three star-devils were no longer at the entrance … and Mr. Géricault was nearly outside!

Then something dark stepped in his way. It was a star-devil but not Dr. Trug. He was taller for one, and crowned with an unruly shock of bright, orange-red hair.

"And just where were you planning to go with that?"

He asked.

Chapter Fifteen

For one interminable second, Gerysalon stared contemptuously into the depths of Natonoc's glasses.

Then, with a curse, he thrust the screaming child into the linewalker's arms and shoved past, heading out onto the flat. Natonoc let him go. The others would handle it from here.

"Now, now, it's all right," he said, straightening the boy's shirt. "The bad man isn't going to hurt you any more. Look! There's Mummy! Mummy's here!"

"I don't know how to thank you," Carlina said to him, taking Jonathan into her arms. "I really thought he was going to do something horrible."

"And you're very likely right. But the lad is safe now."

"What happened to your friends?"

"Currently having a little chat with your friend."

"What are they going to do?"

"Something horrible." He gave her a thin smile.

He followed Carlina back to her table, where Sophia was making it very plain that she didn't appreciate being abandoned. Thus preoccupied, Carlina handed the baby back to Natonoc while she comforted her daughter.

"Under a bit of stress are we? No, darling, not the glasses!"

"What? Oh, I'm so sorry!"

Hastily, she took back her son and began settling him

into his berth on the ride-a-long. Thanks to Gerysalon's attentions, however, the security straps had been completely pulled out.

"It's always something," she grumbled.

"Allow me."

Natonoc reached into his coat for the roll of duct tape he kept in the lower pocket. Folding a long strip in half, he wrapped it around a strut and then across the child, securing it with another piece of tape. A similar strip replaced the shoulder harness.

"May not be pretty, but it will hold him until you can get it properly repaired," he told her. "And I'm afraid I've been rather remiss as to introductions. You may call me Mr. Archer."

"Carlina White, but you probably knew that already."

"Indeed. I met your husband just this morning."

"You did?"

"It appears our friend decided to wage an assault on two fronts today." Briefly, he told her about the planted schematics on Nigel's computer.

"It's Christina all over again," Carlina muttered angrily. "Only this time it'll be Nigel in prison. Wonder how long it'll be until they decide to cut out the auxiliaries and just arrest *me!*"

"You making deals with the Devil again?" Christina called out, coming over to the table with Robyn in tow.

"In a manner of speaking," Carlina told her. "Christina, meet Mr. Archer."

"My pleasure."

"So, what happened to the other guys?"

"Currently indisposed. They're involved with a medical emergency."

"Now, there's a topper!" Christina laughed. "Star-devils on a medi team!"

"I fear you misunderstand," corrected Natonoc. "They are not responding to an emergency. They are creating one."

Meanwhile, Robyn was very nearly standing on Natonoc's shoes. He was looking up at the linewalker with all the intensity of a snooker player lining up a difficult shot.

"Are you really the Devil?"

"Robyn!" His mother admonished.

"Well? Are ya?"

Natonoc knelt down until he was at eye level with the child.

"There are people who like to call me the Devil," he told him. "But my friends call me 'Mr. Archer.' Are you my friend?"

The boy stood there a moment as he thought this through. Then he held out his hand.

"I'm Robyn!"

"Pleased to meet you."

"Your eyes really glow?"

"Now that is a very personal question," Natonoc said, standing up again. "And I believe it's time we were going."

Carlina was more than happy to be out of the ice cream parlour. She was walking so fast that even Natonoc was finding it difficult keeping up with her. Admittedly, his stride was being cut short by Robyn, who was practically glued to his left knee. The boy was running along sideways, with his head turning at odd angles, trying to catch a glimpse behind the glasses.

"Ya know? It's kinda funny when you think about it," mused Christina. "That we go around calling you guys devils when you're nicer than the regulars."

"You've never wondered about that?"

"About what?"

"That you can get away with calling a vytoc the Devil," Natonoc said. "And to do so practically to his face. Could you imagine doing that to a Facilitator? To the Cat?"

"Now that you mention it, it does seem kinda queerd. Why is it, you think?"

"Psychology, Chris," said Carlina. "When you have people under your control who might not wish to be under your control, you want them to think of your enemies as being their enemies as well. After all, your enemy is their potential ally."

"Except I wouldn't call us the enemy, exactly," Natonoc suggested. "Think of us as the Ethics Committee."

"You're the enemy all right," quipped Christina, with a smirk.

They were passing the theatre now. Natonoc waved a hand toward Christina's name on the marquee.

"I hear you've gained some acclaim for your role as Lynessa.

"Yep-pers!" Christina said, proudly.

"A very popular show, *Wider Horizons*. I believe there's a least one production a year, either televised or on the stage."

"Yeah. I was on television just a few months ago. And the Rep is thinking of doing a brief run later this year, during the elections."

"Interesting timing. But I wonder...how much do you *really* know about the Tyler rebellion? What do they tell you in school, for instance?"

"Pretty much just show us *Wider Horizons*," Christina said. "It doesn't get much mention, really."

"So everyone simply accepts the stage production for the actual history?"

"I guess so. Why?"

"Well, what would you say if I told you Lynessa was, in fact, Vyn Tyler's sister rather than his wife."

"No way!"

"Oh, yes! And they leave out some other important little nippits as well: namely the star-devils, who ensured that certain Council members were in no condition to cause trouble on the day Tyler brought his accords before the assembly."

Christina moved her mouth, but nothing was coming out.

"Of course, mentioning our involvement would override the basic premise of the play, i.e. that humans can take on the vytoc -- all by themselves -- and win.

"Lastly," he added. "Tyler never pointed a gun at anyone. That would have served little purpose against a Council made up entirely of vytoc."

"Cassi told me something about that once," said Carlina. "But Mr. Géricault kept giving her a different story. To be honest, she never knew quite what to believe."

"I'd say *not* Mr. Géricault," Christina snorted.

"Igetthebutton! Igetthebutton!" Robyn cried out as they approached the verticals. Natonoc resisted the urge to call the lift himself and let the boy do it.

He even held him up to punch in the number on the destination keypad.

"Eight! Five! Go!"

"I see you know your numbers."

"I can count to hundreds!"

"Bear in mind," Carlina said with a smile. "That means counting up to twenty and then repeating again with the word 'hundred' after each number."

"Sounds like he has a bright future in government

accountancy ahead of him."

The lift finally opened out at the 85th level, where Coriolon was waiting for them, stretched out on a nearby bench.

"Dr. White, Miss Manning, I'd like you to meet my colleague, Mr. Cornelius."

"Pleased to meet you," Carlina said, and then a look of grave concern crossed her face. "You weren't planning on following me home, were you?"

"We might be doing a lot more than just following," Natonoc explained. "I fear your family is in great danger; today's little incident only the beginning. Therefore, I and my brethren plan to keep a close watch, until such time as we can provide a resolution to the larger issue."

"The larger issue being Mr. Géricault."

"I fear it could take a while."

"My husband is not going to like this."

Indeed, the other Dr. White was decidedly not happy about coming home to find a star-devil sitting on his living room sofa, children on either side, reading a story book.

"What the ruddy *hell* are you doing here?"

"Reading *The Little Fraidy Cat*," Natonoc replied, showing him the book. "And, if you don't mind, we've almost reached the gripping conclusion."

"Fraidy puts the fire out!"

"Now, now. We mustn't give away the ending."

"This is Mr. Archer, dear," Carlina said, coming in from the kitchen. "We had another run-in with Mr. Géricault and this time he tried to go after Jonathan. Mr. Archer intervened, so I've invited him and Mr. Cornelius to dinner."

"Whatever for? They don't eat."

"We do so!" Came a voice from the kitchen. Coriolon appeared in the doorway holding a large spoon. "You like goulash, I hope? We'll let you have the chunky bits."

"So, where's the other one?" Nigel groused. "Asleep in the baby's bed?"

"Dr. Trug had to be elsewhere," said Natonoc.

"Medical emergency," added Christina.

"As long as one of them's doing something useful," Nigel grumbled, slouching into a chair. He listened in stony silence as Natonoc read on about the neurotic kitten, who overcomes a fear of heights to save his family from a kitchen fire. In a truly Titanian plot twist, the cat douses the fire by knocking out a hose from the hydroponic garden.

"But the Little Fraidy Cat was afraid no more. He hopped up on the windowsill and curled himself up. Just like any other cat! The end. Now, if you will excuse me, I need to have a word with your father."

"We have nothing to discuss," said Nigel.

"Au contraire! We have plenty."

"There is nothing you can do, or say, or *give* me that will make me cooperate with your lot in any way."

"Is that so?"

Natonoc reached into the pocket of his waist coat and pulled out a pair of small envelopes. Nigel's eyes widened as they slid toward him, across the sofa table.

"Tea?" He asked, as if mentioning something sacred. "Real tea? God, it's been ages since I've had a proper cup."

"Of course, if I really wanted to tempt you, I'd have brought along a few pints and a fried haddock. But these fit easier in the pocket."

"Don't forget the chips," Nigel said, tossing the tea bags back to Natonoc. "Nice try, though."

"Please understand, I have no designs on your wife or anyone else in your family. Nor do I care one whit if a native Latebran ever becomes a vytoc or not. However, you must understand that you are up against a very formidable enemy whose opinions in this regard are notably different from my own. If it helps, think of me as an advocate for your defence. Your solicitor, in other words."

From the coats draped over the back of the sofa, he pulled out a pair of net-phones.

"One for you and one for the missus. Should you find yourself in a tight spot, don't hesitate to call. Our codes are listed on the side: mine is VL8 and Mr. Cornelius is VL1. In the meantime, I and my colleagues will be guarding your wife at all hours."

"Is that really necessary?"

"Yes," Natonoc said, firmly. "After what happened this afternoon, we can only assume that our Mr. Géricault is not only obsessed, but enraged as well. You and your family are very much in danger."

"Would he kill her, do you think?" Nigel wondered. "He's always been so keen on making her immortal."

"Mortally wounding a person and then joining them to the Matrix when they beg to live is not unheard of," Natonoc told him. "But it is very much against our laws. Sadly, recent evidence would suggest that our friend is already operating outside the bounds of those laws."

"And you're the vytoc constabulary, are you? Fair enough. Give Carlina a phone, but as for me..."

"You'll take the phone!" Carlina called out from the kitchen. "And you're not leaving this house unless it's in your satchel!"

"Her Majesty has spoken," Nigel sighed, taking the phones just as Robyn ran past with an armful of books.

"I'm glad we could settle this amicably," Natonoc replied as the boy shoved another book into his hands. "And now it seems we're about to embark on another thrilling adventure with that inestimable explorer, Howie Hupert! And today's episode is...*Howie Goes to the Hydro!*"

"As you can see, there is now a phone in each of our satchels," Nigel was saying as Natonoc continued reading. "Happy now?"

"We need them," came Carlina's voice from the kitchen.

"There'll be snowfall in Hell before I use it!"

Giving Natonoc a vicious look, he stomped off to shut himself in the bathroom. Dinner was nearly over before Carlina could coax him back out again.

Chapter Sixteen

"Forget it, Ger. They're staying."

"They are meddling in my affairs!"

"And as far as I'm concerned, they can keep meddling!"

Kittyvoc continued down the corridor, shouting the occasional command into his communicator, while Gerysalon followed at his heels like a small, yapping dog.

"You do understand, I was viciously assaulted by those barbarians! In public, I might add."

"Yet you still manage to chase after me," Kittyvoc sighed. "Natonoc must be losing his touch....Cat to Foz, is the parking zone secure?"

"Jus' squeaky, mate," came Fosteperon's voice through the earpiece. "I'm keeping Connor and Tullen at the ramp. An' it's linewalkers to the portal level, with Talon in an ambulance, an' Tonners chasing it! "

"Good. Keep a guard on every stairwell, and I want you watching the lifts. Anyone tries an override, I want them going straight to you. Shutdown in five minutes!"

"Roger that!"

He stepped into an open vertical, but the doors wouldn't shut. Instead, they shimmied back and forth, as Gerysalon contradicted Kittyvoc's commands. The battle of wills proved too much for the system, however. The override engaged, cutting off the power and leaving Kittyvoc standing in the dark; going nowhere.

"I demand to know why they're here!"

"We were getting low on pudding."

"The real reason, Cat!"

"If you insist!" Kittyvoc snarled, pushing his way out of the dead elevator. "We can talk in my office."

On the comm, meanwhile, Kosk was reporting that the main entrance was secure and all human non-essentials had been accounted for. Fosteperon responded with an order to have them sent home, while Jensen reported that the Prefect was secure in his quarters.

And Portysanon's in his office, Kittyvoc said to himself, as the last of the reports came through. *Let's hope he has the sense to stay there.*

And to think, the day had started out so normally! The only unusual notice to be found on the overnight report, was the arrest of a group of University students for petty vandalism in the Bridges district. While students were known to get into a certain amount of mischief, property crimes were generally something you found in the lower levels. Go anywhere below level 15 and you'd find that most of the windows had been replaced with grills of wrought-iron.

At the Bridges, the kids had defaced a few statues and broke some windows, but nothing was damaged that couldn't be easily fixed. Still, the flat was a city showplace, and it didn't take long for the police to put an end to their game. The kids could expect to spend the weekend in the prison's minimum security level, but they'd most likely be released to their parents before Sunday. At worst, they'd have to pay a fine.

But then somebody dropped a "tip" to a news crew, telling them that the "Titan Seven" had been transferred to the Black Tower. Almost immediately, people began holding demonstrations in the major shopping districts. Kittyvoc noticed that the signs – most of which accused the Facilitators of oppressing the city's young people – looked far too well made to have been drawn up at the spur of the moment. Odder still, the demonstrators were choosing to keep their distance from the Black Tower, itself. A spokesman claimed they feared reprisals, but the Cat had a hunch ...

There were rumours of riots breaking out. The police had summoned the Security Services ...

And Kittyvoc was not about to play along! Instead, he called in his agents, including those off duty and two of the three linewalkers. He'd been putting everyone into position when Gerysalon decided to stick his nose in.

Entering his office, he gave the door a vicious swing. But Gerysalon managed to catch it before it hit him in the face.

"You really want to know why I brought in Natonoc?"

"I want to know why Natonoc was in the Communication Center this morning, running a transmission history on *my* communicator. And this on top of that violent and *unprovoked* attack upon my person yesterday afternoon –

one that happened at the Bridges, I hope you know. A very *public* part of the city! It is exactly this sort of barbarian behaviour that encourages disrespect, and ultimately rioting, such as we have seen today! These malformed malcontents are an abomination to our kind and I demand that they be permanently banished from Latebra ... permanently!"

"They are here investigating a murder," Kittyvoc replied, calmly. "They go wherever their leads take them."

"That hardly excuses their abuse of one of the city's top officials! Besides, what need do they have in investigating the Liaison Office? Murder is a human crime."

"Really," Kittyvoc said, leaning back in his chair. "So tell me ... what *do* you know about David Cawthorn?"

"He was a Councilman. Got mugged on the way home from work."

"And that is all, Monsieur Liaison Officer? A man is shot in the parking zone of the main government office tower and you just shrug your shoulders and call it a mugging?"

"Humans die incredibly easily," said Gerysalon. "And with all the maintenance ladders in this city, it's difficult to keep any area completely secure. Besides, any fool knows government officials have money."

"Not to mention bodyguards," Kittyvoc added. "Who, in this case, seem to have been derelict in their duties. Nor was our mugger particularly adept at *his* profession either. Councilman Cawthorn was found with all his bank and ration cards intact."

"He did have political enemies."

"As do we all," Kittyvoc said, smiling. "Though one does begin to wonder who this *particular* enemy might be. Cawthorn was, after all, a close friend to Vyn Tyler."

"You're not accusing me are you?"

"No, I'm already well aware that you were at a meeting of the Hydroponics Association on the night in question," he acknowledged. "On the other hand, there have been some very odd coincidences over the years involving the Cawthorn family. It makes one wonder if they are being targeted by someone with a longer than average lifespan."

He gave Gerysalon a pointed look.

"You might remember the first attack. It came just days before Tyler's famous coup. Cawthorn's brother was tortured to death and his sister-in-law was dosed with vytasynene. She managed to survive, but the attack helped to foster distrust between Cawthorn and Tyler at a critical moment in their plans. Small wonder, then, that Cawthorn was left behind when Tyler and the others went into exile.

"The person responsible was never caught. But witnesses describe a vytoc wearing dark glasses."

"A linewalker, then," fumed Gerysalon. "All the more reason to keep them out of the city."

"There are doubts that a real linewalker was involved."

"You said you had witnesses."

"Yes, except one witness in particular could not give us a direct answer, which is generally the case when someone given vytasynene is uncertain of the truth. Masie Cawthorn could only say she was attacked by a vytoc, nothing more."

"Maybe she didn't get a good enough look. Anyway, that was years ago. I fail to see how it relates to our current situation."

"Because our mysterious linewalker has turned up again, in two more attacks on the Cawthorn family. The first occurred about two years ago: Jason Van Eman, Daniel Cawthorn's half-brother, was shot in an altercation on the thirtieth level. Witnesses say the ghost child died trying to protect his brother from ... a vytoc wearing dark glasses!"

"Like I keep telling you..."

"And I'm telling you the *real* linewalkers have no idea who it could be! Portal Control has no record of any linewalker crossings to Latebra outside of those already known to the Security Services.

"Plus, there's the curious matter of the weapon used in both the murder of Van Eman and the elder Cawthorn. Ballistics tests would suggest a Luger pistol. I find that an interesting detail considering our linewalkers generally prefer Walther makes -- either the PPK or P-38."

"They prefer anything that shoots," huffed Gerysalon. "Surely they'd carry a Luger if they had one!"

"I was thinking more in terms of your Luger."

"Fosteperon owns one as well. It in no way implicates..."

"Then where is it? Talonyvoc says the gun is not in your office, nor your quarters."

"He searched my quarters? He had no right..."

"And according to your communicator logs," Kittyvoc continued, pulling out a folder. "You have been unusually generous to a couple of my men."

"The Liaison Office is allowed to give bonuses where it sees fit."

"Yes, provided the money comes from the government account and goes for services clearly rendered. These, however, involve money transferred from your private account without any manner of reason given."

"Done for matters which are of no concern to you."

"Sure about that?" Kittyvoc said. "The records show 525 sestri transferred to the account of Agent Lewis on the day Christina Manning was arrested (always suspected you had a hand in that). Then there's the 888 sestri given to Portysanon on the day of the Prefect's assassination. *His* records show it was withdrawn *in cash* the very next day. Now, 888 sestri makes for a very heavy valise! So, where exactly was this money going ... or, should I say, to whom?"

The response was a stony stare.

"Well? I'm waiting."

Gerysalon started to open his mouth, but any words spoken were immediately drowned out in a sudden cacophony of alarms. Nevertheless, this seemed to cheer Kittyvoc to no end.

"Ha! I was right!" He cried, shutting off the nearest klaxon. "A little ruckus to bring out the guard while the real trouble sneaks in through the back door!"

"What are you ta..."

"We're under attack, Ger!"

Setting aside the discussion at hand, Kittyvoc switched on his communicator. Through the earpiece, he could hear Fosteperon calling for reinforcements to guard the stairwells at level 85. This would mean the action was either on that floor or the one below. From there, the closest entrance would be the service dock and parking zone on level 50 -- a good thirty-four levels farther down.

That would make for a miserable hike if the insurgents took the stairs. He wondered how long they'd been climbing. And did they get a chance to rest before meeting up with Fosteperon? This could be over with quickly if the Resistance was out of breath.

"Foz! It's Cat! Are they still in the stairwell?"

"They're in stairs A-2. I'm at B-2 and..."

A popping sound in the background was answered by a flurry of curses, followed by a series of much louder popping sounds. Something unintelligible was being shouted in the background, before another agent's voice came over the comm:

"Cat! It's Peters! Foster's down!"

Then Fosteperon cut in:

"Sweet dingos! Don't know what they hit me with but it shattered my hip! They're headed south on A. If you come down stairs 6, I think you'll have 'em."

"Are you moving, Foz?"

"I'm managing, but I'm going on holiday after this if you get me meaning."

"Understood. Cat on the way!"

Kittyvoc grabbed his MP-40 which sat in a rack on the side of his desk. It was already loaded with a 30-round clip. Almost as an afterthought, he pulled a revolver from a nearby cabinet and handed it to Gerysalon.

"Here. Make yourself useful."

Gerysalon started to protest, but Kittyvoc wasn't listening. He was nearly to the stairwell when he heard Fosteperon's voice in his ear again:

"Got one! And they're runnin' now, by God! Peters! Keep 'em in A! Cat! Get down here, dammit!"

"It's Cat. Coming down now!"

Moving quietly but swiftly down the stairs, Kittyvoc could hear the gunfire echoing up from level 84. He pushed his way past the stairwell guard just as the door opened below. A warning shot from the MP-40 and the door slammed shut again.

Knowing the enemy was on the other side, Kittyvoc came through the door firing, keeping his body low to slide neatly into a side corridor. He caught a glimpse of three figures diving to the floor of corridor 6, while he took cover in A.*

Gerysalon followed, but had neither the training, nor the reflexes to cope with an urban gun battle. This time, the Resistance got the first shot.

A barrage of very undiplomatic French echoed through the halls. Kittyvoc turned back to find Gerysalon lying on the floor, a wide crack in his skull.

Glancing down the corridor, he saw what looked to be a shoe disappearing around a corner. Then its owner appeared, jumping out with gun at the ready. But the Cat was quicker. One shot and the gunman fell, tossing the rifle over to someone unseen.

Just like the Red Army. Means they've got more men than guns.

"It's Cat! Targets at 6-C! Box 'em in, Foz!"

"Roger that!"

Meanwhile, the fallen figure was still moving.

"Well, well. If it isn't Silas Doering!"

"Eat death, Tocker!"

---

* In Titanian skyscrapers, corridors running north/south are designated by letters, while those running east/west are numbered. In the lower levels of some of the largest skyscrapers, which can be small neighbourhoods in themselves, corridors may have names as well.

"Always," Kittyvoc smiled, before turning back to his comm:

"Peters! It's Cat! Can you spare me a medi team? I've got a downer at 6-C."

"You can have Kymsen and Lewys," Peters answered. "And it looks like our friends have split apart. We're chasing them out of rooms, now. Funny thing is, nobody's armed!"

"One of them is. Ger's down."

"Understood. Call when you're moving"

Kittyvoc turned to his wounded comrade:

"You okay, Ger?"

"Splitting headache. Got any tape?"

Tape, particularly duct tape, is the primary means of first aid among vytoc, and Kittyvoc always kept a few rolls in an old bread bag he wore on his belt. Tearing off a few strips, he wrapped the tape tightly around Gerysalon's head. Since vytoc are immune to infection, all that mattered was that he keep all the pieces together to expedite healing. Anything missing could regenerate, including the entire head if necessary.

"Cat! It's Foz! We've got the lot down at C-2 and I'm puttin' 'em in the common room to cool down."

"It's Peters! We're not done yet, Foz! Still two running – last seen at D-4!"

"It's Cat! We're coming up 6! Try to pen 'em in at E-5!"

"Understood!"

"Roger that!"

"Think you can run any?" Kittyvoc asked Gerysalon.

"I'll try my best."

They came up the hall where Kymsen and Lewys were tending to Silas Doering.

"Get him to an infirmary room and keep him under guard," Kittyvoc said in passing.

"Understood, sir!"

At the end of the hall, another figure darted out, heading towards the stairwell door. Kittyvoc fired a warning, and the figure hit the floor, rolled upright, and fled. It was a move one could expect from someone with actual military training. Like a Newcomer, perhaps?

Hello, Dr. Nielsen!

Nearing the end of the hall now, Kittyvoc turned to Gerysalon and pointed up another corridor.

"Run up and see if you can catch 'em at 5!"

There were more shots down the next hall. Peters must be at the other end. Kittyvoc jumped out just as the insurgents made another go at the stairs.

"Halt!"

The man in front had the gun. He fired, but the shot went wide. Kittyvoc didn't give him a second chance.

"Lor! ...ohSHIT!"

Dr. Nielsen caught his comrade as he fell; easing him to the floor, though it was clear the man was already dead. He looked up at the Cat, grief and anger plain on his face.

"He was just a kid!"

"That's the way of war," Kittyvoc told him, coolly. "Young men die. But give me the gun and I promise the killing will stop."

"Like hell!"

Dr. Nielsen picked up the rifle but he didn't try to fire it. Instead, he ran back down the corridor, cradling the gun in his arm.

"You there! Halt!"

Gerysalon was at the intersection, with Peters stepping out a little farther up the hall.

Dr. Nielsen started to bring the gun up, but fired before he aimed. The round caught Gerysalon in the left knee, nearly cutting his leg in half.

Returning fire as he fell, Gerysalon managed to miss Dr. Nielsen and instead, hit Kittyvoc in the chest. Before either could recover, Dr. Nielsen pulled the cover off a maintenance shaft and jumped in. Agent Peters was first to reach the opening.

"Which way is he going?" Kittyvoc asked, trying to dislodge the bullet.

"Down, sir."

"Good. The Devil can have him."

He walked back to where the latest human casualty lay.

Laurence Wittyn. There'd be no need to call for a medi team this time.

"One dead, and it's a Councilman's son. Looks like the Liaison Office is going to be busy for a few days."

"Actually, it's two dead sir," Peters said. "Foz got one at the start and Kymsen confirmed it – and one other wounded."

"What about ours?"

"Steffens and Maak are wounded but not badly. But Lenzel got hit by the rifle. We're not too sure if he's gonna make it or not."

"And two vytoc incapacitated."

Kittyvoc spoke into the comm:

"Kymsen! It's Cat! Please state your status. Your downer is now a priority prisoner. Is he secure?"

There was no answer.

"Kymsen? Can you read me?"

A moment later and another voice came over:

"Cat? It's Kosk! I found Kymsen lying in the hall on level 95. He's all alone and looks pretty beat up!"

"Take him to the infirmary and tell me when he's conscious."

"Understood."

"Foz? Did you give the medi team use of a vertical?"

"Yeh, what with two downers an' all. Thought I had it set for 90, though."

Although he was speaking through the comm, Fosteperon's voice could also be heard coming down the hall. He hobbled up to them, using a custodial mop as a crutch.

"Skiver!" He called out to Kittyvoc, as he passed Gerysalon. "How come you still got a leg to stand on?"

"It's those cat-like reflexes," Kittyvoc replied, smiling. "And it seems our Mr. Doering was equally lucky."

"Think he had a friend waitin' for 'im?"

"What I think is that agent Lewys had best be in my office in five minutes. We're overdue for a little chat."

"Roger, that."

Chapter Seventeen

"The Devil can have him."

Phil was climbing down the maintenance ladder as fast as he could, the Cat's words ringing in his head. The star-devils were down here somewhere, though just *where* was anybody's guess. It was hard to be certain of anything in the dark.

He wasn't quite sure just how far he'd come, but every so often he'd come across something that felt like an entrance. Assuming there was only one per floor, he guessed he was at level 79 – or possibly 80. He wasn't sure if he'd missed one or not.

The worst part was the noise. He was making too much of it. Doering's rifle lacked a shoulder strap and it was no easy task to hold it while climbing. It clanged and clattered against the ladder rungs to such an extent that he was certain it could be heard all the way up to the Prefect's office.

At least he'd managed to shoot the Canuck. Nigel would be happy to hear that, though he'd probably leave out the bit about *where*.

Another entrance. This was either 74 or 75.

Wincing as the rifle hit an already bruised thigh, he quietly cursed Doering and the whole blasted Resistance. He'd told them from the beginning that the plan read like a bad episode of *Tower Eighteen,* and he was not particularly happy about being proven right. Worse, he'd probably be taking the fall for the whole thing, provided he got out of here alive.

It had been a cock-up from the start: Saylor had bribed several police officials into giving their group access to the Black Tower via the bridge at level 42. Most had been "arrested" for vandalism earlier in the day and Phil, along with Dr. Swendon and a few interns, had shown up later in response to a supposed "medical issue" among the prisoners.

Naturally, Saylor himself kept to his office, leaving the operation to Silas. Unfortunately, the younger Doering chose to ignore Phil's warning regarding the use of things electrical when vytoc are present. Silas bypassed the stairs, herding them all into a single elevator for the ride up to the Prefect's office.

Miraculously, they got all the way up to the 78th level before the vytoc cut the power. Now stuck between floors, it was up to Phil to get everybody out and into a stairwell – which was where they should have been from the beginning!

Most were able to escape before the Australian pried the doors open. Lionel (bringing up the rear and possessing their only other gun, a Vyn 12 pistol) was pulled out and arrested, along with another of the University kids.

With the tockers in control of the elevators, Phil knew the cause was already lost. Silas, however, insisted that they go on anyway, arguing that his father had everything under control.

skull in the other.

"Hookay," Phil said to himself. "Maybe it's a good thing I've never met a lady vytoc. They look even nastier than the guys!"

He edged closer to the strange "tomb entrance." A coldness emanated from it, as though from a cave. But this was a funny level to be finding a cave at. What was it really? And what had the star devil meant by "exactly where *he wants to be?*"

He felt a glimmer of hope.

"Not much of a space port," he said to the figures on the walls. "But I'm not gonna complain."

Stepping back a few paces, he made for a running start, and jumped through...

Darkness.

He did not so much enter the portal as become enveloped by it. His skin burned with a bone-chilling cold and his lungs struggled for air -- but there was none save his own exhale. Panicked, he tried to turn back, but he couldn't move in any sort of real direction. He was like an astronaut, completely weightless and floating in a black void, but without the benefit of spacesuit or tether. Blindly, he reached out his arms, flailing for the entrance; certain in the knowledge that if he didn't get out of here immediately he was most definitely going to die.

Then something grabbed him by his shirt collar and

pulled him backwards. Next thing he knew, he was lying on the floor of the museum room, gasping for breath. The German star devil was kneeling beside him.

"Here. Drink this," Dr. Trug said, giving him a small bottle of vitamin water. "We'll give you a moment to recover and then we'll be going."

"What was that place?"

"It's a little difficult to explain. The portal's internal dimensions don't actually extend through what we perceive as 'space.'"

"The way home?"

"In a manner of speaking."

"I wanna go home."

"I'm sorry, but that will not be possible."

Phil wanted to argue, wanted to punch the star-devil in the nose, but he knew it was pointless. This was it. The end of the line. No going home. He would never see Lara again. He'd never see his mom, his dad, or even the dog again ... ever. The realization cut deep and it hurt.

"Ready?"

"I think so."

He finished his drink and slowly stood up. He gave no resistance as the star-devils led him back through the hall and into the waiting elevator. He had to admit, there were times when he had relished the idea of being a political prisoner, but not like this. Not after a failed coup and *definitely* shadowing Carlina for most of the evening, and the rest he spent teaching Robyn how to make paper boats. Made a miserable mess of the bathroom. On the other hand, we've never had an easier time getting the boys to take their baths."

"Can't believe you let them around your children."

Nigel finished his sandwich, brushing the crumbs from his hands.

"'Let' has nothing to do with it," he said. "They've taken it upon themselves to be the guardians of my wife and family. And if you have any ideas on how to change a vytoc's mind then, please, do tell."

"Oh, I don't know," Phil said. "I told the Kraut to take a flying leap just this morning."

"And he leapt?"

"In a manner of speaking," he smiled. "Came by just as I was leaving for work, insisting that I head out to Tylerville right that very minute. Even said he'd escort me to the gate! 'Course, I couldn't leave just then – had to go up to the lab for my memory bars if nothing else. And how could I run off without one last lunch, yeah? Besides, I've got Bull and Serena comin' over this afternoon to take care of my stuff. So, I told Dr. Frankenstein to take a hike ... and he did."

"Do you think that was wise?"

"Why? You think I'm gonna get pinched again?"

"Actually, I'm more concerned about your Resistance friends," Nigel said, worriedly. "You did say Swendon threatened you, plus we already know they were planning to make me the scapegoat in all this. Herr Doktor could be aware of something you're not."

"Now don't you go taking their side," Phil scoffed, playfully shaking a finger. "Doering ain't Al Capone, trust me! I mean, anyone who goes up against Vytoc HQ with only a handful of kids and a small calibre rifle ain't gonna do anybody much harm."

"Bloody well hope you're right."

"Relax, Nage. I'll be okay."

They paid their bill and headed back onto the flat, stopping at last by the big public lifts stationed next to the hospital.

"Y'know, it's gonna feel strange livin' on the ground again," Phil said, hitting the call button.

"Feeling nostalgic?"

"Ironic, ain't it? But this place does kinda grow on you after a while. Hey, be sure to write, okay? You can always send a letter through Laas if the post don't cooperate."

"Don't suppose your friend, Laas, could be hired out for a weekend? I could do with a holiday."

"That's the spirit!"

"Mind you don't get into any trouble at the gate."

"Don't worry 'bout me," Phil said, patting his breast pocket. "I got my papers!"

The lift opened up and, after a final farewell slap on

Nigel's shoulder, Phil stepped in. He gave a salute through the glass as the car headed downwards and out of sight.

Godspeed and, for Heaven's sake, don't do anything rash!

Returning to the hospital, Nigel couldn't quite shake the sense of loss that was settling over him. It was worse than watching his friend board an aeroplane.

Funny that. It was farther from London to Southend than it was from Titan to Tylerville. Yet here he was, moping about as though Phil were going all the way back to America again.

Above him, a domecock fluttered from an overhead rampway. It tried to catch itself on a window ledge, but was too weak to hold on. With a strangled squeak, it dropped directly in front of Nigel, landing at his feet. It struggled for one last breath, trembled, and lay still.

"Poor little thing," said a woman passing by. "They try so hard to get in here, only to discover it's a death trap."

"Works both ways," Nigel muttered, but the woman had already gone. Gingerly, he stepped over the deceased creature, and into the lobby of the hospital.

Chin up, man! It wasn't an omen!

His mood didn't get any brighter once he reached the lab.

Four of their interns, along with Dr. Swendon, had been arrested in the raid on the Black Tower, and it was anybody's guess when --or if-- they would be returning to work. Now that Phil was gone as well, the laboratory felt downright deserted.

He forced himself into his latest project, hoping to smother his anxieties with work. But it was no use.

"Problems, Doctor?" Dr. Spaulding asked, as Nigel sat there, giving his microscope the hundred yard stare. "It's Phil, isn't it?"

He nodded.

"It's nothing but pins and needles until I hear he's safe in Tylerville. I apologize if I'm not quite a hundred percent today."

"None of us are," Dr. Spaulding admitted. "And with six people gone, I don't know which way to turn. Tell you what: let's just close up early today, get some rest, and start over fresh on Monday. How does that sound?"

"Doctor, if you were a woman I'd kiss you!"

Dr. Spaulding laughed.

"Do give Carlina my regards. Now, get outta here, and don't show your face 'til Monday!"

Despite the worry that continued to nip at him, Nigel felt a certain amount of relief as he left the hospital. Finding a rare seat on the helix train, he headed home in good spirits. As luck would have it, the intercity championships would be starting this evening. He'd be able to sit back and numb his brain with soccer while he waited for word from Phil.

On the other hand, the apartment was a lot more

crowded than it used to be.

It had only been three days, but the star-devils had already entrenched themselves. Dr. Trug and Mr. Archer alternated days and nights, while Mr. Cornelius came and went, invariably showing up in time to help make dinner. In this, Nigel's feelings were decidedly mixed. The bastard was a damned good cook.

Something else occurred to him as he unlocked the door: it might have been wise to call ahead and alert the "home guard" to his change of schedule.

"You're home early," Mr. Archer said, tucking his pistol back into its holster.

"Nothing's wrong, I hope," added Carlina from the kitchen.

"Let's just say it was a less than productive afternoon."

"Da!"

Jonathan ran up to give his father's leg a bear hug.

"Hullo, sport!"

He reached down to pick up his son, but the boy dodged his grasp. With a squeal, he ran off to hide behind his mother.

Nigel tried not to take it personally. Ever since the incident at the ice cream parlour, only Carlina and Mr. Archer had been able to hold Jonathan without provoking a screaming fit. It was in marked contrast to his more affectionate older siblings. And on that note...

"Where's Robyn?" He asked, heading into the kitchen.

"Chris took him out to get some new clothes for school," Carlina said, busily plucking the feathers from Gaila's latest gift. "I'm assuming you saw Phil on his way?"

"To the lift, at any rate. Seems he's not too keen on escorts."

He opened the refrigerator, hoping to grab a bottle of cider.

"What the devil?"

"You rang?"

Mr. Cornelius was standing at the counter behind him, chopping vegetables for the slow-cooker. He grinned wickedly as Nigel pulled a brown glass bottle from the fridge.

"Beer?"

"Took a nip over to Colchester this morning," the star-devil explained. "Picked up a few things."

He reached in to grab a parcel that was wedged between the chicken stock and goat marinade. As it passed his eyes, Nigel noticed it was wrapped in the London Times.

"My God! Fish?"

"Dover sole to be exact. I bought five, expecting Dr. Nielsen to be joining us, but since that does not seem to be the case, you should have plenty left over for later."

"Don't know if I should feel grateful or just slap you with it."

"How about having yourself a beer, putting your feet up, and enjoying your time off," said Mr. Cornelius, gently pushing Nigel back into the living room.

Which, of course, meant being back in the same room as Mr. Archer.

Of the three star-devils, Nigel found Mr. Archer to be the hardest to take. No doubt, it was partly because the vytoc was a fellow countryman, but mostly it was the accent. Mr. Archer had a voice that spoke of Eton and Oxford, and afternoons at Ascot, and possibly tea at Buckingham Palace.

Yet, here the man was, perfectly content to sit on Nigel's middle-class sofa, reading an Agatha Christie novel, while Sophia manacled his legs together with a chain of 'Connect-O-Blocks.' It didn't seem right, somehow.

And the beer, surprisingly, hadn't been over-chilled. No doubt it was Mr. Archer he'd have to thank for setting the temperature in the refrigerator's beverage compartment.

"First time in my life, I've wanted to read fishwrap," he said, conversationally. "It's been so long, I've completely lost touch. I don't even know who the Prime Minister is!"

"Edward Heath."

"Never heard of him. Chelsea keeping up in the standings?"

"They've fallen behind a bit," admitted Mr. Archer. "But you'll be happy to know, they won the Cup a few years ago."

"They did?"

"And England got the World Cup in '66."

Nigel mused over that for a moment.

"Mr. Archer?" He asked, thoughtfully.

"Yes?"

"When you see Mr. Port again, tell him I'd like to kill him.... Mind if I turn on the telly?"

"Go right ahead. There's nothing on."

"Oh, I don't know. It's an election year. There might be something worthwhile on channel one."*

> Next up on Politics Today: our exclusive interview with Councilman Terryl Wittyn, who says he will remain in the Mayoral race despite the tragic death of his son in last night's coup attempt. But first, here's Lucas Pearson to give us the latest on the aftermath, and how this sudden upsurge of Resistance activity could affect the campaign...

"I'd have thought you'd be trying to get your mind off things."

"In a way, I am," Nigel said. "By letting the newsreader worry about it. Let the whole sorry business hit the news, and it seems less real somehow. Just another show, and better yet, none of my concern."

"As if using a staged coup to promote a political campaign sounded real to begin with."

"You think that's what it was?"

"Most certainly. Any real insurgency would have had

---

* Channel One was the government network, usually broadcasting speeches and Council debates. Most Titanians only watched it during the election season, when some effort would be made to keep the programming interesting.

some outside organization behind it, ready to take control once the government fell. However, the Prefect is nothing more than an auxiliary power here, meaning that even if the coup had been successful, it would not have led to any *actual* change of government. At best, it would have enhanced Councilman Wittyn's reputation for being anti-Facilitator, since the news of his son's involvement, as well as Doering's, would become the main topic for gossip throughout the city. Or, to put it another way, what occurred yesterday was nothing more than the government poking itself in the eye on a dare.

"Think for a moment, what would happen if a member of parliament shot the Queen. Would it seriously affect the governing of England? Of course not! Still, it all makes for decent theatre, particularly if you're trying to distract the voting public from more serious issues."

"Hate to admit it, but you're probably right. Even Phil suspects they were set up somehow."

"He's quite correct in that."

"But why?"

"To keep people from noticing how corrupt the system has become," continued Mr. Archer. "Flog a handy scapegoat, and the people willingly vote against their own best interests. We've seen it happen all too often on Earth.

"Unfortunately, in this case, the chosen scapegoat is not as harmless, as some would like to believe. You understand, the Tyler Rebellion was a long time ago and men have short memories. People have forgotten how powerful our kind used to be. They see the Facilitators of today as mere supervisors, or perhaps a means for acquisition. We moderate debates and bring bread to the masses. So, in their eyes, we've gone soft; fit only for target practice.

"Sadly, there are vytoc willing to exploit such forgetfulness, even to the point of allowing a raid on their own headquarters. Encourage an uprising, you see, and you'll win the right to crush it."

"And in so doing, dispense with the Tyler Accords," Nigel mused. "The Prefect's setting fire to the Reichstag, in other words."

"It's not the Prefect," said Mr. Archer. "He actually prefers the status quo."

"So who's behind it, then?"

"Do I really have to tell you?"

"No, I guess you don't," Nigel sighed. "Though I don't see how any of this involves my wife."

"It doesn't," acknowledged Mr. Archer. "For while the Resistance is seen as nothing more than a political pawn, his attacks on Carlina are personal."

"Because of Cassandra." It wasn't a question.

Nigel gazed listlessly at the television. He understood now, why he and Carlina had never been given the option of moving to Tylerville. It simply wouldn't be far enough.

219

The sound of the door unlocking brought him back to the living room, while Mr. Archer came to his feet. But it was only Christina and Robyn, returning from their shopping trip.

"Lookit my shoes!" Robyn cried as he blurred past.

Christina flopped onto the sofa beside Nigel. Before he knew it, she had commandeered the video wand.

"Just so you know, I'm changin' the channel once *Fenton's Landing* comes on."

In standing, Mr. Archer had snapped his chains, meaning Sophia was now busily gathering the remnants. Jonathan toddled up to gather a few loose links of his own. He wandered off again with his head adorned in a colourful circlet.

His sister was not amused. With a shriek of fury, Sophia went for the boy. She didn't just walk, she *ran*, pushing Jonathan to the floor and taking the block-ring for herself. Proudly, she paraded past, as though having regained a crown.

"If I had known that's what it was going to take," Carlina said, rushing over to comfort her crying son. "I'd have had him a long time ago."

Sorry to interrupt, Mr. Councilman, but we have just been handed breaking news regarding a double homicide on level 63. Police have confirmed that one of the victims is Silas Doering, son of...

Nigel stared at the screen in shock as the newsreader continued.

"Good God, 'Lina! They've killed him!"

Chapter Nineteen

"I don't have the gun, all right!"

"Then where did you hide it?"

"I just told you! They took...it...from...me!"

Phil was trying very hard not to shout, but his voice was rising, along with his temper. On the communicator screen, Saylor Doering remained as impassive as ever. Not for the first time, Phil wished he could just reach in and smack the man upside the head.

"I'm afraid you don't understand," Doering was saying. "I have plenty of contacts in the Black Tower. Had the Security Services captured our gun, I would most certainly have heard about it. Yet the gun remains unaccounted for."

"Yeah. These wouldn't be the same sources who assured you we could take out the Prefect with only one rifle and a handful of unarmed men, would they?"

"Obviously a miscalculation."

"Bullshit, Saylor! They're either incompetent or they set us up!" Phil was practically up against the screen now, despite the knowledge that this was distorting the view on the other end. Considering where the camera was placed, Doering was likely listening to an extreme close-up of Phil's left eyebrow.

"Not to mention they misjudged the Cat from the get-go! What makes you think the devils didn't just hide the gun away somewhere and not tell anyone?"

Saylor was giving him the sort of smile that, in Chicago, generally accompanies a trenchcoat full of watches.

"I know our ways may still seem alien to you," he was saying. "But we Titanians utilize Facilitators even when we resist them."

"Oh, then that settles it. We *were* set up!" Phil fumed. "Now, if you don't mind, I've got company to get back to."

"Of course you do!" Doering's smile grew even wider. "Good day, Doctor."

"Good-BYE!"

"If you had activated the privacy setting," Bull said from the kitchen. "He wouldn't have been able to call you."

"Yeah," Phil said, pressing the appropriate button on the video wand. "Just didn't think about it . Had other things on my mind, you know."

"You probably should go now," Serena said, coming out of the bedroom with a large box. "We can take care of the rest."

"Aw, I ain't scared of that idiot," Phil said, pulling his exosuit from the hall closet. "Talk about all bark and no bite! Hell! If I'd have known he'd been dealing with tockers from the start, I never woulda joined up! ... Got everything?"

"Not really," Bull said, bringing out a box from the kitchen. "Most of your pots and pans are too small. We can still use the plates and silverware, though."

"Not a problem. We'll just leave the rest for the next guy."

To be sure, Phil had never gone out of his way to make the little apartment liveable. The furniture was all Facilitator-issue: a single table with a cracked top, two battered chairs, bookcase, chest of drawers, two twin beds, and an absolutely hideous, striped sofa with an old journal propping up one leg. The walls were windowless and bare, save for a calendar and an abstract ceramic plaque with ROBYN engraved in large letters on the corner.

With some reverence, he took the plaque from the wall and sandwiched it between a couple pairs of trousers in his cycle-trunk.

"And that's all that's going in there," he said, struggling with the latch. "You guys get everything else. Hope the clothes aren't too big."

"Big's all right," Serena said, taping up the boxes. "Big stuff can always be cut down and the scraps made into quilts and baby clothes. Nothing gets throwed away where we come from!"

Now there was only one thing left to pack. He began searching around.

"Sell-don! Heeeere, kittykittykitty!"

A dark blur shot out from behind the sofa and hid itself in the bedroom. Serena followed, emerging a short while later with a large ball of fur struggling in her arms.

"You guys don't eat cats, I hope."

"Don't worry, he'll be fine," Serena assured him. "We always need cats for the hydro, and around the goat pens, to keep the rats out. He'll have plenty to eat and lots of new friends to play with."

"Good to know...'cause I'm gonna miss this guy."

With one last pat on the head, he helped Serena put the cat in the vet carrier.

"And that'll be Muncie with the hauler," he added, as the doorbell chimed.

Only it wasn't.

Immediately, the ghost children took cover. Bull ducked behind the kitchen counter, while Serena hid behind the sofa. It was uncertain whether Silas Doering saw either of them as he walked in through the door.

"Planning to go somewhere, Philippe?"

"What's it to you?"

"Oh, nothing," Silas said, innocently. "It's just that we'd hate to have you run off without returning what is rightfully ours."

"Look, Silas. Like I told your Old Man, I don't have the gun. The tockers took it, okay!"

"You must think I'm a street-level shit digger to believe that."

Silas had been keeping one arm behind his back. Now he brought it up, revealing the pistol in his hand. It wasn't his usual Vyn-12, though.

Probably one of Antony's new prototypes, thought Phil, even if it *did* look rather like an old luger.

"Where is it?" Silas demanded.

"I don't know!"

"Goat-shit!"

"He's telling the truth!" Serena cried, coming out from behind the sofa. "The gun isn't here!"

A confused look briefly crossed Silas' face. Then he brightened up again.

"It's with your Newcomer buddy, isn't it?" He grinned. "The one with the tocker bodyguard!"

"Leave Nage out of this! He doesn't have it either!"

"Shut up."

Silas was too close to miss. Three quick shots, and Phil was sent careening backwards. He was dead before he hit the floor.

"You didn't hav'ta do that," Serena said, quietly, kneeling beside Phil's body. "He didn't even have a gun!"

"No, he didn't. That's why he's dead."

"He was our friend."

"So?"

Silas had barely said the word before his body suddenly contorted sideways. He let out a horrible scream, firing the pistol in random directions as his arms flailed and twitched. Serena flattened herself out on the floor, until the pistol dropped from the man's hand. It wasn't long before Silas fell as well, convulsing violently.

With vytasynene, death is certain but not necessarily quick. Nearly ten minutes would pass before Silas Doering finally lay still.

"There are consequences when you hurt a ghost child's friend," Bull said, holstering his dart gun. "Any street-level shit digger would have told you that."

"Now what?" Serena asked.

"We wait 'til Muncie gets here an' call the police," he told her, carefully removing the dart from the body. "Then I think we'd better run."

Chapter Twenty

"What is this? Pink aspic?"

"Beet and cheese casserole. The Carolsyn's brought it."

"Laas was here? I never saw him!"

"That's because you were too busy talking with the Mortons. By the way, what did they bring?"

"Cheese, and a loaf of meschel bread."

"I thought the bread was from next door."

"No, that was the biscuits and ... what are *these*?"

"Bereavement squares. Remember? You had them at Cassi's funeral -- and you *liked* them."

"Had I been drinking at the time?"

"*Ni*-gel!"

From his post in the living room, Natonoc quietly eavesdropped on the bickering in the kitchen. It had only been nine hours since they'd first heard the news about Dr. Nielsen, and the shock and grief had already given way to the cataloguing of casseroles.

Titanians traditionally gave food to the bereaved, but the surge of sympathy that evening had caught the Whites entirely by surprise. Nigel never realized it before, but their friends regarded him as Phil's brother, making him the logical recipient for condolences. He'd been receiving visitors until well into the night.

By now, the children were in bed and, gradually, the conversation in the kitchen moved to the bedroom as well. Another hour later, and the house was quiet. Though whether that meant the principle adults were asleep, or just staring up at the ceiling, was anybody's guess.

Natonoc remained in the darkened living room, keeping himself occupied with a penlight and the latest by Asimov.

From the bedrooms came a rustling and a muffled cry. The baby most likely. He put down his book, and wandered over to the White's nursery annex.

Since Jonathan needed a vytasynene injection every two hours, his bed was kept separate from his siblings, so as not to disturb them during the necessary nighttime interruptions. His room, in fact, was the former family office space; set somewhat apart from the master bedroom. Chances were good the boy had not awoken his parents.

"Something amiss, young man?"

"Muah?"

Jonathan was standing up in his crib, legs dancing, and looking very much like a penned-in puppy. Natonoc's nose told him the rest.

"Time for a change is it? Well, come along then and we'll get you sorted out." He pulled the boy out of the crib and carried him over to the changing table.

"Here we are! No...not the glasses! Oh, all right then,

take them."

"Gee!"

"Yes, they're green. And if you don't fuss about so, they'll stay green."

"Gee!"

Trying to keep as quiet as possible, he fastened the safety straps and began looking around for the usual manner of supplies. It wasn't easy in the dark, but he managed to find the wet-wipes and a clean diaper. He'd just found the talcum powder when the light came on.

"You're a man of many talents," noted Carlina, standing by the switch in her dressing gown.

"I'm not completely inhuman," Natonoc said, looking around. Only too late, did he remember who had his glasses.

"Oh! I'm terribly sorry," he apologized, eyes turning a deep blue. "I know my appearance can be disconcerting."

"Well...Jonathan doesn't seem to mind,"Carlina said, recovering. "I...I'm sure I can learn to live with it."

"That is most obliging of you."

Getting back to the task at hand, Natonoc cleaned the baby and pinned the new diaper while Carlina took on the thankless job of dispensing with the old one. Though it was a little ahead of schedule, she gave Jonathan his injection as well.

"Mommy, I'm hungry..." came Robyn's whine from the doorway. "Wow! Your eyes really do glow!"

"We're two out of three," Natonoc said, wrenching his glasses from Jonathan's grasp.

"Three for three," Carlina corrected him, as a squeal could be heard from the adjoining nursery. "And I suppose there's nothing wrong with an early breakfast. I could make some meschelmash."

"Yeah!"

"But we have to be quiet. We don't want to wake daddy."

"Provided that daddy was asleep to begin with." Nigel said, joining the party with Sophia in his arms. "Shall we invite the neighbours in as well?"

"I'm hoping we're at capacity," Carlina smiled, heading for the kitchen. "Do you eat meschelmash, Mr. Archer?"

"Provided it has plenty of cream, yes."

"And you, Darling?"

"None for me, but thanks all the same."

Sophia and Jonathan were set down to join Robyn in pestering their mother in the kitchen. Natonoc returned to his post, but not before Nigel discovered the book he'd been reading.

"Phil used to read this stuff," he said, thumbing through the pages. "Even named his cat after some character or other. Never saw the appeal myself."

"The genre can be an acquired taste," agreed Natonoc,

declining to add that if Nigel didn't like books of the sort, then he could kindly give that one back.

It wasn't long before the sweet smell of meschelmash began to waft through the apartment. But the cooking time proved longer than the children's attention spans, and soon all three were back in the living room.

"Mr. Archie? Will you read us a story?"

"Certainly. Have you got a story for me to read?"

The boy gave him a magisterial look.

"Wait *just* one minute," he said, solemnly.

While Robyn ran back to the nursery to get a book, Natonoc engaged Sophia and Jonathan in a form of vehicular 'catch,' wheeling Kitti back and forth across the living room floor.

"You know, for an Eton man, you make a pretty good nanny."

"Noticed the tie, did you?"

"I would think changing nappies and reading storybooks to be a bit below your station," said Nigel.

"Lots of things are below my station," Natonoc replied, as Sophia toddled off to find something less acceptable to play with. "In fact, I find my station to be rather dull, which it why I pay it no mind."

"You're certainly the odd duck, Mr. Archer."

"Thank you, Doctor."

Robyn came running back then, arms laden. But

before Natonoc could begin reading, there came a sudden, ferocious pounding on the front door.

"Security Services! Open up!"

"What the devil?" Nigel glanced over at Natonoc but the linewalker just shook his head. Whoever was outside, they weren't vytoc.

Vytoc would at least have been able to activate the lock.

Having no desire to get into a gun battle with so many humans present, Natonoc began looking around for a less dangerous weapon. Thinking fast, he scooped Jonathan into his arms just as the door split apart. A man in a jade green uniform forced his way in, followed by four regular policemen. To his relief, they were armed with nothing worse than stun wands.

"We're here for Dr. White. He's under arrest."

"By who's authority?" Natonoc asked, coolly.

"By order of the Security Services."

"You're lying. The Cat has issued no such order."

"It's by order of Special Investigator Alrund, and I have the warrant right here," the agent blustered. "Any questions, you'll have to take it up with him." He motioned to the policeman closest to him.

"The man on the sofa."

"What about..." The officer waved his wand in Natonoc's direction.

"He isn't our concern."

Another policeman, this one wearing sergeant stripes, started to step forward. Natonoc moved to block him.

"I'm sorry, but I cannot allow this."

"Then you're under arrest as well," the agent said. "Take him, Tyndahl!"

Sgt. Tyndahl took another hesitant step forward. With perfect timing, Jonathan chose that same moment to make another attempt at Natonoc's glasses. The dark lenses fell away, revealing eyes glowing stoplight red.

The policeman immediately holstered his stun wand.

"Forget it, Mack. This ain't my pay grade. C'mon, boys! We're outta here!"

"You can't do that!" Wailed the agent.

"Watch me."

"I give the orders here!"

"Fine. You arrest it." Sgt. Tyndahl turned and walked out into the hall, followed by the others.

"You come back here right now!" The security agent screamed, chasing after his support. "I'll have your commissions for this!"

"Think he'll be back?" Carlina asked, worriedly.

"Not without his backup," replied Natonoc, his eyes already an amused yellow.

Setting Jonathan down again, he found his coat and pulled out his net-phone.

"Calling your friends?"

"Calling the Cat," he said, entering the contact code.

"It appears we must facilitate some repairs to your entryway."

Chapter Twenty-One

"Come on, Cat! I haven't been gone a week! You didn't have to go an' change everything!"

"Had to take the opportunity as it arrived," Kittyvoc said, handing Fosteperon the latest duty rosters. "Try to clean out the riff-raff before Gerysalon wakes up and starts causing trouble again."

Resignedly, Fosteperon flipped through the rosters.

"We're rid of Alrund, I see."

"For the time being, anyway. He'll be back, you can bet on it. But he's out of our hair for the weekend, and that's what's important."

Fosteperon gave him a puzzled look.

"What's on for this weekend?"

"Christina Manning's début at the Rep for one thing -- *Girl in Tower Seven*. Going to be a grand gala, with a public meet-and-greet for all the mayoral candidates. Need I explain farther?"

"Got an extra ticket, have you?"

"Not exactly."

Kittyvoc passed him another roster. Unlike the others, which had been printed off the computer, this one was hand-written on a scrap of stationary paper. It listed only six names.

"Green Room party?"

"Certainly not your typical deployment," Kittyvoc

agreed. "At least, not for us. And not all of them are ours to start with. You'll notice Silas Doering has been crossed out."

"Another attempt on Christina, or one of the candidates?"

"Six of one, half a dozen of the other, though I think Erkenbeck's the likely target. With Cawthorn gone, he's the only one left in the race who doesn't have ties to Saylor Doering. On the other hand, Natonoc has informed me that there's a warrant out for Dr. White again. That's *Mister* Dr. White, by the way, though that doesn't necessarily mean his wife isn't a target as well. Nobody's actually seen the warrant, but Lewys tried an arrest the other night."

"S'when's the funeral?"

Kittyvoc laughed.

"Let's just say Lewys should count himself lucky he caught Nat holding a baby instead of a gun."

"Pity that," Fosteperon said, folding the rosters and sliding them into his knapsack. "Would love to see Natter send Lewys home in a snuff box. Might bring Alrund down a peg or two."

"Returning to the theatre," Kittyvoc continued. "I'll need you to draw up a new roster, this time with people we can trust. You'll be happy to hear we've got Gooch on loan as substitute Special Investigator. With luck, he can block any attempts by Alrund to make the fête a police matter."

"Alrund's in the regulars now?"

"Portysanon called in a favour," sighed Kittyvoc, adding a mild oath in Serbian. "Lewys went with him. Chief probably thought he was getting a two-for-one deal, though after Saturday's little tête à tête, he's no doubt reconsidering that decision."

A hesitant knock drew his attention to the door.

"Come in."

In walked a pale-complected man in his fifties, with a stocky build that suggested he'd been working at a desk too long. He wore an ersatz uniform of black trousers and a jade green jacket. The latter was at least one size too small.

"'Allo, Gooch!" Fosteperon said, cheerfully. "Ready for duty?"

"Already on," he replied, pulling something out of his work satchel. "In regards, at least, to the murder of Silas Doering." He placed a pistol on Kittyvoc's desk.

"Where did you find this?" The Cat asked, grabbing the pistol and checking the serial number.

"Long story," Gooch said. "But your man, Alrund, has been a royal knife in the cogwheel ever since he crossed the Bridge of Tears. Last Friday, for instance, he managed to be first at the scene at the Nielsen homicide. Before the forensics people could even open their kits, he was running off at the mouth to the news people; telling anyone who'd listen that both victims were shot and a possible gunman was still at large! It was Cassandra Manning all over again, especially when the coroner told me Silas Doering tested positive for vytasynene. Now, I can't *prove* Alrund tampered with a crime scene, but I find it interesting that he had *this* in his locker. Cornelius already confirmed it's Facilitator property."

"The gun that killed Cassandra?" Fosteperon wondered.

"Perhaps. Maybe," said Kittyvoc, stashing the pistol behind a secret panel in his desk. "This *is* Ger's gun. However, in regards to the late Miss Manning, a gun of *any* type would have been of little consequence."

He leaned forward, lowering his voice to a near-whisper.

"You may not know this, but the official coroner's report was found to be a fake. Gooch here is probably one of the few still around who remembers seeing the original."

"Cassandra wasn't really shot," confirmed Gooch. "According to the coroner, cause of death was electrocution."

Fosteperon's eyes grew wide. He started to say something, but let the matter drop. There were some things one simply didn't discuss with humans present.

"So, all we need to find is a pair of dark glasses," he said, strategically changing the subject.

"I'm one ahead of you," Kittyvoc replied, pulling out a pair of shades from a desk drawer. The style was about a hundred years out of date, but they were definitely linewalker glasses.

"Now, where'd you get those?"

"Alrund's desk. Where else?" He answered with a Cheshire grin. "Gooch isn't the only one who can pick a lock."

"Hold it," exclaimed Gooch. "Does that mean Alrund was involved with the Van Eman case as well?"

"Just an accessory, really," Kittyvoc explained. "It's the Liaison Office that's pulling the strings in this puppet show. But I'm pretty confident Alrund is the one who shot up Port's Cadillac."

"Y'know," Fosteperon added, putting on the glasses. "If you trim the hair just right, you wouldn't know Mr. Port from Mr. Cornelius. Think I'll start calling Cor 'Starboard' from now on. ...How do I look?"

"Blind."

"Right," Gooch said, his hand on the door handle. "Think I'll be getting back to work. There anything else I need to be on the lookout for?"

"Just keep an eye on the police department for us," Kittyvoc told him. "And report any suspicious moves by Alrund and company, particularly with regards to doctors named 'White.'"

"Understood, sir."

"So, it's all over but the shouting," Fosteperon said, as the detective took his leave. "Which reminds me..."

He rummaged around in his knapsack, finally pulling out a slightly crumpled roll of parchment.

"Met up with Martynoc on the way to the portal. He said it was important this got to Natonoc as soon as possible."

"Oh, dear dear me," Kittyvoc grinned, looking at the seal. "The last brick is falling into place!"

"An injunction by the Council?"

"Almost as good," said Kittyvoc. "It looks like Our Lady is about to show her hand. If this is what I think it is, the whole Manning business will either be put to rest or..."

"It's gonna be blazin' fireworks!"

Fosteperon stood up, swinging his knapsack onto his shoulder.

"Guess I'll be gettin' on those rosters," he said. "Nice doin' business with yer."

"I get the glasses, Foz."

"All right. If you insist."

All alone now, Kittyvoc took out his stress ball and idly bounced it against the far wall. Whatever judgement lurked within the Lady's parchment, one could guarantee it would send Gerysalon into a raging fury.

He put on the glasses, looking at his reflection in the dark mirror of his communicator screen. He was facing a very tough call:

Did he dare bring over more linewalkers?

Chapter Twenty-Two

"Right. Bring up Subject 6 and, I think ... Subject 11."

An intern by the name of Ries, clicked his compustylus at Nigel's computer. Two images appeared, showing detailed MRI's of stomachs bloated by tumours. The two were very similar. One might almost think they were identical.

"No, it's not 11," Nigel said, sorting through sets of tissue samples. "Try Subject 12."

Another stomach appeared.

"That's it. And I believe that's about the lot....Send the packet to Judi and, if you would, walk these up when you're finished." He indicated four sets of samples.

"If you don't mind my asking," enquired Ries, as he transferred the data, "Why are we sending cancer subjects to epidemiology?"

"Because they're not cancer. Bring back 6 and I'll show you."

Ries did so. One could safely argue that the stomach *looked* cancerous. Certainly, there was a large mass nearly blocking the entrance to the duodenum.

"Our little friend, Tullermicium Fibrostomiasis," said Nigel, grimly. "You may know it better as Tully's Goitre. Colony usually develops either in the jowl or oesophagus, however, a few years ago, we discovered a Beta strain, which sets up housekeeping in the duodenum. Little buggers have proved a headache ever since, as the Tully-Beta mass is nearly indistinguishable from a late-stage mescheloid tumour -- as you can see. Worse, the colonies actually thrive on kessil-derived chemo. One misdiagnosis, and the cure kills the patient."

"Isn't Tully's caused by flatworms?" Ries looked a little ill.

"Despite the many rumours to the contrary," Nigel explained. "One generally gets it from contaminated water, most often unsanitized river water, which has helped to give it a reputation for being a street-level disease. But you can contract it just as easily from an unclean hydro. Tricky part is getting people to accept that, since it's the rare tower-dweller who'll admit his hydro's getting on the mossy side. So much easier to blame an outbreak on unscrupulous restaurant chefs. However, I've seen my share of hot springs flatworms and I assure you, nobody in his right mind would eat one, no matter how well it was prepared."

"If it's in the hydros then, does that mean we could be facing an epidemic?"

"Which is why we're sending these to Judi," Nigel smiled, handing Ries the samples.

The intern hurried off on his errand, leaving Nigel to sort through the remaining samples. Tulermicia were among the few Latebran protozoans able to infect humans, although to be strictly technical, they were fairly benign. Unfortunately, if the colonies grew too large, they could suffocate their host – or block the small intestine, in the case of Tully-Beta.

It was a small relief to have found only four cases in the current test sample. Problem was, he only had seventeen subjects to begin with. One never saw large sample groups here, but then Latebra's entire human population numbered less than 100,000; making it very difficult to find accurate statistical measurements for anything. Nigel had found this to be a major stumbling block in the progress of medicine here. He hated to admit it, but you could argue it justified bringing in "updated" oncologists like himself ... and Phil.

"Dr. White! Dr. White!" Ries burst through the door at a full run, nearly sliding into a table as he skidded on the linoleum. "It's the police!"

"What's going on?" Dr. Spaulding asked from his office.

"Police," said Ries, gasping to catch his breath. "Saw them by the verticals ... heard 'em asking directions ..."

"This have something to do with Phil?"

"No, it bloody well *doesn't*," Nigel growled, pulling the net-phone from his work satchel. He had Mr. Archer's code already punched in by the time the officers entered the lab.

"Police! We're here for..."

"Yes, yes, I'm right here. No need to shout," he said,

holding up a finger for silence. "Ah...Hallo, Mr. Archer? This is Dr. White. Seems I've found myself in a spot of trouble...."

"Whossat you talking to?"

"My lawyer...er, hold on...yes?" Nigel handed the phone over to the sergeant. "I believe he'd like a word with you."

"He would?" Confused, the policeman took the phone. "Uh, hi...what?...He's bein' arrested...for the Nielsen business, that's what...well, he's being taken to headquarters for questioning...Alrund, that's who. Look, you want the doctor, you'll have to talk to Lt. Alrund!"

He shut off the phone.

"We'll be taking this, as well as checking your authorization. Something tells me you ain't a baby doctor."

"Don't suppose any of you are with the Security Services?"

"Not us, pal. You got lucky this time."

"In that case, I demand that you take me to the Cat immediately."

The policemen seemed to find this amusing.

"Buddy, you ain't demanding nothing," said a second officer, applying the handcuffs. "Now, move!"

It was a most humiliating procession, as the hospital was a close knit community and Nigel knew most of the people they passed recognized him. Still, he kept his head up, hoping that he was sending the message that 'here walks an innocent man.'

The police van was parked outside the lobby entrance, and Nigel was shoved in with little regard for the difficulties inherent in boarding a vehicle with your hands tied behind your back. Inside, there were no seatbelts or restraints of any kind, making the trip to Tower 4 a separate hell all its own. The driver seemed to take great pleasure in sharp turns, and Nigel was knocked sideways with every twist in the rampways; occasionally being thrown to the floor if the turn was hard enough.

Shaken, but still upright, he was led out of the van. To his horror, he found himself, not at the general entrance on 45, but the maximum security terminal on level 39.

This was a fortress within a fortress. The van had parked deep inside the tower, and Nigel was herded through a bulletproof chute to the processing rooms. Every policeman he saw – including the lady at the desk – was armed with a stun wand.

It was a gauntlet of degradation. He was forced to change into a prison jumpsuit and submit to a body scan, plus the usual mug shots and fingerprinting. For the first time in his life, he would have a criminal record, and they hadn't even charged him with a crime!

Finally, the processing clerk handed him a card listing all of his belongings. What it didn't list was his name. From now on, his identity would be the number on his jumpsuit.

"Keep this. You'll need this upon release," she said.

"Provided, of course, you *are* released," added one of the officers with a grin.

"Take him to 42-6 for questioning."

Three levels up. Naturally, they made him take the stairs.

The interrogation room wasn't much to look at, but Nigel had seen enough old movies to know you don't need more than a single chair to give a suspect a rough time. This chair, however, looked like something out of a mad dentist's office. He was strapped in, leaning back, and facing a single bright light that snaked down from the ceiling. All he needed now, was a couple of thugs in trenchcoats and fedoras.

"I demand that my lawyer be present."

"Mr. Alrund *is* your lawyer."

Laughing at his own joke, the policeman stepped back into the hall, locking the door behind him.

They wouldn't come right away, of course. *Trying to foster panic,* he thought, bitterly. But he was far from panicked -- he was bloody furious! He should have been home by now, getting ready for Christina's play, not sitting here in a cold room, while some damned vytoc played cops and robbers with him.

The hum of a door lock activating heralded the arrival of his inquisitor. Mr. Alrund was nearly as tall and slender as a vytoc, with a pale complexion, close-cropped hair and perfectly manicured fingernails. He wore plainclothes and sensible shoes, but there was something about him that suggested jack boots.

"Good evening, Doctor White. I'm sure you know why we brought you here."

"Haven't the slightest," Nigel told him. "But I do know my rights. I demand to have council present before questioning."

"That would be the right of a Citizen, Doctor."

"I *am* a Citizen."

He was on the alert now. Had someone altered his citizenship status in some way? And did he really need to ask?

"Perhaps you weren't aware," Alrund said. "But your citizenship was revoked some eight days ago. This session is being conducted under Newcomer code. Legal representation is not necessary."

"In that case, I demand a Facilitator present. A member of the Security Services preferably."

"Doctor White, I *am* the Security Services." He gave Nigel a cruel smile. "And we are wasting time. Now, tell me. Where were you last Friday at about 15 hours?"

"On my way home from work. Spaulding shut down early that day."

"When was the last time you saw Dr. Philippe Nielsen? I believe he was a colleague of yours."

"He was my closest and dearest friend."

"Was he?"

"We had lunch together at the Underpass," Nigel told him, irritably. "It was a send-off, you see. He was leaving for Tylerville that afternoon."

"So, you knew he'd be home."

"Of course. Though I don't know what that has to do with anything."

"Dr. White, we know you left work at approximately 14:45, and we have witnesses who saw you on level 65 thirty minutes later..."

"They are mistaken. I took the helix directly to 85. I never went lower."

"Do you recognize this gun?" An image appeared on the wall in front him.

"Old Earth weapon. German by the look of it," Nigel shrugged. "Couldn't tell you much beyond that."

"But it *is* your pistol."

"I do not own a pistol."

"You admit you stole it, then."

"I never!"

"Do not lie to us, Doctor. We know all about your people and their knowledge of firearms. We also know there was evidence found on your computer that would suggest you are an experienced weapons-maker."

"That evidence was planted. Ask the star-devils if you don't believe me."

"Star-devils are not the most trustworthy of vytoc," Alrund said, dismissively. "Getting back to the matter at hand: on the day before he was murdered, Dr. Nielsen stole a very valuable new rifle – a weapon capable of actually murdering a vytoc. Dr. White, where is that weapon?"

"How the bloody hell should I know?"

Mercifully, any farther questions were drowned out by the frantic blare of alarms, followed by a sudden pounding on the door. Clearly annoyed by the interruption, Alrund went over and let the officer in. Nigel recognized him as being the security agent who had tried to arrest him a week ago.

"What's going on?"

"All hell's broken loose," said the agent/officer. "We gotta get outta here!"

"I am conducting an interrogation."

"Better just leave it." He glanced over his shoulder at something outside, then hurriedly shut and locked the door.

At that moment, the light snapped off.

Then the lock on the door *exploded*.

Acrid smoke wafted through the room, stinging the eyes. Alrund flicked on a penlight, allowing for just enough illumination to reveal Mr. Archer coming through the doorway. His glasses were off and his eyes glowed scarlet. In the smoke and shadows, he truly looked diabolical.

The agent/officer was closest to the door. He drew his stun wand, but it had little effect on the vytoc. In return, Mr.

Archer gave him a glancing blow across the head, hard enough to knock the man unconscious.

"Are you *quite* finished?" Snapped Alrund.

"My client is being questioned without suitable representation," Mr. Archer said, his eyes cooling to a yellowish orange. He handed Alrund a business card. "Nathaniel Archer at your service. Solicitor and Newcomer advocate."

Alrund gave him an icy glare.

"Whatever a solicitor may be, I am more than certain that there is no such thing as a Newcomer advocate. Now, if you are done with your little tantrum, I demand that you leave. You are interfering with a murder investigation here, and you can trust your superiors *will* hear of this!"

Without a farther word, Mr. Archer pulled out his pistol and fired once into Alrund's chest. The former Special Investigator fell to the floor, blood glistening in the feeble torchlight.

"Consider yourself lucky," Mr. Archer said, returning his gun to its holster. "*My* superior would have throttled you with your own intestines, cut off your head, and kept the skull for a souvenir."

He lit a torch, shining even more light onto the ghastly scene.

"Are you all right, Doctor?"

"I'm fine," Nigel said, looking down at what remained

of "Lt." Alrund. "You didn't have to do that, you know."

"We are called 'devils' for a reason," replied Mr. Archer. "Though to be honest, he was a greater devil than I."

"Still, to kill him like that? In cold blood?"

"Ask any vytoc, Doctor, and they will tell you star-devils are the most cold blooded of our kind. But I assure you, I do not kill without good reason. This *gentleman*," he said, giving the body a prod. "Had, on numerous occasions, demonstrated a casual indifference to the rule of law. You're not the only innocent man he's tried to pin a murder on."

"Then he should be arrested," Nigel argued. "Given a proper trial."

"Before what judge?" Countered Mr. Archer. "All magistrates here are appointed by the Liaison Office."

"Mr. Géricault … "

"Due process can be difficult when the corruption starts at the top," Mr. Archer said, unbuckling Nigel's restraints and helping him out of the interrogation chair. "Your clothes are in the hall. Get yourself changed, but be quick about it. You were due at the theatre ten minutes ago."

"Bugger that," Nigel grumbled. "Carlina must be frantic by now."

"Dr. Trug is with her. He will have told her you were delayed."

"Good." He located the pile of clothing and other personal items, and began changing out of his jumpsuit. He didn't bother asking how Mr. Archer came by his possessions, though he suspected it had something to do with the alarms going off. Hopefully, nobody had been injured too badly.

"Bastard picked a hell of a time to do this," he growled, tying his shoes. I'm going to look a proper git going to a gala in this suit."

"Can't be helped," Mr. Archer said, putting his glasses on. "We're late enough as it is and, under the circumstances, I would not want to keep your wife waiting."

Once they were out in the corridor, Mr. Archer turned the lights back on. The entire level appeared deserted. Obviously, word had got around as to just who was down here. A few policemen appeared later, but no one challenged them – except for an officer standing guard at the bridge to the Black Tower. Nigel recognized him as Sgt. Tyndahl.

"Heard the shot," he said as they approached. "You left a mess for us, didn't you."

"Just preventing a larger one," replied Mr. Archer.

"Who was it?"

"Alrund."

Sgt. Tyndahl thought for a moment; then stepped aside and opened the gate.

"Not one of ours," he shrugged. "Carry on."

Nigel felt almost giddy crossing over, though he knew he was far from in the clear. He'd been around Titan's theatre scene enough to know Mr. Géricault never missed an opening night, and it was anybody's guess what he was planning for this one.

As could be expected, the lift was open and waiting for them. Once inside, he noticed the destination readout flashing '50.'

"We'll have to go higher than that if we want to get there with any speed," he commented.

"This is the car park."

"Have a race car on reserve?"

"Almost as good."

Mr. Archer directed him to the Firebird, which sat gleaming in its stall like a metallic thoroughbred.

"Other side, Doctor. It's American."

"Oh, yes. Of course."

Nigel slid into the passenger seat while Mr. Archer started the ignition. The cavernous parking zone reverberated with the unmistakable roar of an Earth-made engine. It was enough to bring tears to the eyes – or perhaps that was just the exhaust.

In a matter of minutes, they were charging up the Periphery at 60 miles an hour; sending the smaller, Titanian vehicles swerving to the side lanes to keep out of their way.

"While I have you here," Mr. Archer was saying, as the upper curve of the dome drew nearer. "Don't suppose you'd mind hearing another vytoc proposition?"

"Suppose I would."

"How would you feel about returning to England?"

"Right. I'm listening."

Chapter Twenty-Three

"*Girl in Tower Seven,*" read Nigel, thumbing through the program. "Gynstra's classic retelling of Duvel's *Dome Windows,* as updated for modern tastes. Sounds like one of those atrocities they do to Shakespeare."

"An apt comparison," agreed Natonoc. "Duvel was Pre-Titan, but his plays remain popular for their universal themes. *Dome Windows* is rather like *Othello* in a way: lust, jealousy, obsession; all leading to a tragic end. Every few years, someone comes along and gives it an update. However, given time, even the updates become a bit dated. *Girl in Tower Seven,* for instance, was written prior to the Tyler rebellion and refers to situations that are no longer applicable. It's safe to assume this will be a modernization of the modernization."

"So, what's it about?"

"Like I said: lust, jealousy, and obsession," Natonoc explained. "Unrequited love and a man's foolish yearning for a woman he cannot have, with a little bit of *Rear Window* thrown in to make things interesting. It begins, you see, with a young man looking out his window at the woman in the tower next to his and subsequently falling in love. The only problem is, aside from a lack of curtains, is that she's already married. However, this little fact does nothing to discourage his advances. So, he plots against her husband, going so far as to hire star-devils to be his hit men. Tragically, the object of his affection is willing to defend her man and ultimately takes the bullet."

"And I'm going to have to sit through this, am I?"

"In that case, you'll be happy to hear we've missed most of the first act. However, I suggest you keep an open mind. The second act is an insult to all that is vytoc. You just might find yourself enjoying it."

Natonoc beckoned to an usher, handing him Nigel's ticket.

"You're not sitting with us?"

"I am needed elsewhere this evening. But I'll see you again at intermission."

With Nigel now safely to his seat, Natonoc wandered around to the usher's nook. This was a tiny room set into the supports of the right balcony, enabling theatre staff to monitor the performances, as well as to keep a discreet lookout for unruly patrons. Tonight, it had been commandeered by the Cat.

"All quiet on the Eastern Front?" Natonoc whispered.

"So far, so good," Kittyvoc murmured back. "But then, I'm not expecting trouble until later. It's the meet-and-greet at intermission, and the party afterwards we'll have to keep a watch on."

"Understood."

In silence, they waited out the first act. Natonoc found Titanian theatrical style fascinating, though it could be hard to handle in large doses. The acting was very broad and melodramatic, reminding him of the silent cinema. It was to Christina's credit, however, that she gave her character certain subtleties lacking in the other performances. If that caught on, he mused, Titan could be seeing the start of a new era.

"Thank God that's over," Kittyvoc muttered as the curtain fell.

"I've always preferred the second act myself," Natonoc said. "Care to go down for a drink? Christina tells me the profits go toward the company's youth program – a good cause, certainly."

"Only if Christina's teaching the course," yawned the Cat, stretching his arms out. "Really, though, I'll have to pass. I need to make another scan of the Green Room and check the perimeter. No rest for the wicked, you know."

With the mayoral candidates out in full stump, the intermission promised to be extra long. Already, the lobby resembled a cocktail party, with people milling about, drinks in hand, while young men with trays of canapés passed among them. The candidates were all wearing hats, and most of the patrons had acquired at least one campaign button.

Natonoc scanned the crowd, found his target, and plunged in.

"Bon soir, Monsieur," he said, coming up to Gerysalon, who was talking to a pair of councilmen. "Enjoying the play? I dare say, Miss Manning has been absolutely riveting tonight!"

"She's certainly a breakout," agreed one of the councilmen. "Girl's got a bright future ahead of her."

"And Mr. Rigar plays and excellent Kynni. One might even feel sorry for the fool. A sad commentary on human nature, don't you think? That a man could be driven to his own destruc ... "

"All right, out with it," Gerysalon snapped. "You want something. What is it?"

"Merely a minute of your time," Natonoc replied, graciously. "In private."

"If you *must*."

Natonoc showed him into a nearby office. Gerysalon was dressed in the short-sleeved formal wear most vytoc call the "Titan tux." A hat, liberally decorated with campaign buttons, covered the wound in his head, while a pair of flared trousers hid the brace on his knee.

"I must say, you certainly look put together this evening."

"I take pride in my appearance," Gerysalon growled, finding a chair. "Unlike some people."

"I was speaking in terms of duct tape. I mean, it isn't everyday you see a vytoc hobbling about with a cane."

"It's a walking stick. A decorative accessory."

"Not for the man who limps," Natonoc smiled. "Now, I admit, I enjoy a gala as much as the next man, but really!

Shouldn't you be in regen?"

"I'm perfectly fine. Now, if you're through insulting my appearance, what was it you wanted to speak with me about?"

"Oh, nothing. Just the play, really."

"In that case, I suggest you find a human to talk to," said Gerysalon, petulantly. "Councilman Marcus seemed more than willing just now. I, however, have more important matters to attend to."

"I'm sure you do," said Natonoc. "But the play is hardly unimportant. In fact, I might even call it an object lesson. One you would do well to learn."

"And what would *that* be?"

"That only a self-destructive idiot would believe a woman should bow to his wishes for no other reason than because *he* fancies her."

"I don't see how that applies to me."

"And obstinacy isn't going to help you, not anymore." Natonoc pulled out the parchment, making sure Gerysalon could see the gold-coloured seal. "As of today," he said. "Dr. Carlina White is no longer your concern. All contact is forbidden and you are to leave her, and her family, alone – by word of Our Lady, Octavianovoc."

Gerysalon took the parchment and looked it over. Then he crumpled it and threw it at a recycling chute.

"Means nothing. She has no power here."

"Better read it again, then. I've been granted absolute authority in all matters regarding Dr. White and her family. If necessary, I can take them well away from here."

"Where? To London? Your beloved doctor would be found out in a day!"

"Dear me, no!" Natonoc exclaimed, smiling. "I'd never take them to London! I was thinking more along the lines of … Montréal."

"And you think I couldn't find them *there*?"

"Been there recently? I'd say it's grown a bit since 1690."

Gerysalon only glowered at him. Standing up, he hobbled to the door, checking his hat and comb-over in a nearby mirror.

"We'll discuss this later … tomorrow, in my office." He started to leave.

"Oh, and one final thing..."

"What?"

"Exactly how *did* Cassandra die?"

Gerysalon did not reply. Instead, he turned on his heel and stormed out, best he could. Natonoc picked the parchment off the floor, smoothed it, and returned it to the pocket of his coat. He waited a few minutes more before heading out himself.

Once again among the campaign crowd, he bought another drink and tried his best to mingle. It wasn't easy.

Titanians tend to be very shy around vytoc, let alone a vytoc wearing dark glasses. It took him a while before he found a friendly face.

"Enjoying the show, Doctor?"

"Insufferable but preferable to prison," Nigel said. Beside him, Carlina was busy chatting with another couple.

"'Lina's been the belle of the ball," he added in a low voice. "These are the Franks – you may remember them from the night Phil died -- and it looks like the Markli's are coming over. Haven't heard from *them* since she got the dose, and ... oh, dear God! What does *he* want, I wonder?"

Natonoc turned around just as Saylor Doering walked up to them. Beside him was an aide holding a large potted marjoram.

"Are you enjoying the show?" Carlina asked, with formal politeness.

"An absolute delight," Doering said to her, smiling and looking surprisingly cheerful for a man mourning the death of his eldest son. "Everyone agrees, your sister is a rising star and truly an asset to the Rep. That said, the committee to elect Terryl Wittyn was hoping that we might give her this little token of his esteem.

"Unfortunately, security has been unusually tight this evening. They're not letting anybody backstage, not even the candidates! Therefore, I was wondering if we might, instead, leave this with you. I trust you can get it to your sister?"

"Chris will be very flattered," Carlina told him, as Dr. Trug took the plant. "I'll be sure to give it to her. You should know, though, she supports Erkenbeck."

"A pity I did not know that," Doering replied with a wink. "I would have brought a larger plant."

After a final round of handshakes, he gave them a couple of campaign buttons before continuing on his rounds.

"With luck, we can get it downstairs before the second act starts."

"It's not going to explode, is it?" Nigel asked as Dr. Trug ran a small sensor across the pot.

"No," he concluded. "It's just a harmless plant."

"Let's get it down to Chris, then," Carlina said, starting out in the direction of the backstage corridors. "Explosive or not, I just want to be rid of it."

At that moment the lights began to flash.

"Five minutes," she noted with undisguised annoyance. "Nigel, you and Mr. Archer can go on ahead. I'll get back just as soon as I've taken care of this. All right?"

"Fine. But please hurry."

Assuring him that Fosteperon was watching the back areas, Natonoc led the reluctant doctor to his seat. He had almost reached the usher's nook when he felt a tug on his coat-sleeve.

It was Special Investigator Gooch.

"Sorry to bother you," he said. "But I believe you own

the black quad-wheeler in the parking zone."

"Why? Has the meter run out?"

Gooch let it go. He'd had enough experience with vytoc, particularly linewalkers, to let most of what they said pass him by.

"Kosk caught somebody trying to take off one of the wheels. Don't think he did too much damage, but you might want to come and see for yourself."

Fac ut gaudeam! Natonoc followed the detective out to the parking zone, where the Firebird sat; its rear end jacked up and three lug nuts lying under the right tyre. A security agent (Kosk, no doubt) was standing beside it.

"Don't think he was expecting anyone to be guarding the parking ramps," he said, as they approached. "Just took one look at me and ran for it. Dropped his wrench, even."

"Did he appear at all familiar," Natonoc asked, picking up the tire-iron.

"Uh, yeah, he did," said Agent Kosk, a little nervously. "He looked a bit like Mr. Port from the Liaison Office."

"Thank you. I'll see to it you get a commendation for this." Natonoc said, twisting the lug nuts back into place. A quick check of the wheel well revealed nothing else out of the ordinary. Portysanon must have been chased off before he could manage any real mischief.

"If you would," he said to the agent. "I'd appreciate it

if you would remain on guard here for the remainder of the evening."

"Sir?" Kosk looked over at Gooch.

"Stay put," the detective told him. "I'll get Jensen to take the zone."

"Understood, sir."

Natonoc had barely pulled the jack away when the great bulk of Portysanon's Cadillac came roaring past. It very nearly clipped the nose of the Firebird before turning up the rampway leading to the theatre entrances.

Then the explosions began.

So that's it!

Running back across the walkway, he met up with Gooch at the theatre entrance. The door had locked itself and the detective was furiously attempting a manual override, without success. Worse, the door wasn't responding to Natonoc either. On the other side, an increasing crowd of well dressed people were pounding on the glass.

"This is no time for niceties," Natonoc said, gently pushing Gooch aside and grabbing a hold of the door. "EVERYBODY STAND BACK!"

A sudden shower of electrical sparks rained down as he pulled apart the computerized locking system; ripping the right-hand door completely out of its frame.

"Easy everybody!" Gooch called out, as panicked patrons began forcing themselves through the opening.

"There's no need to push … come along; keep moving … everyone's going to be just fine..."

"Stay here," ordered Natonoc. "I'll tell Cat you're evacuating at the parking zone. Mind, you don't let too many on the bridge at once."

"What are you going to do?"

"Jump into the breach," he said, turning back to his car. "Via the scenic route."

Chapter Twenty-Four

"Are you all right?" Dr. Trug asked, picking himself off of Carlina.

"Tore my dress," she said, inspecting the seam. "But I think I'm still in one piece. Chris?"

Christina pulled herself out from under her dressing table.

"It's possible my heart *might* start beating again." she assessed. "Snurrgles! Look at my mirror!"

Carlina had reached the dressing rooms minutes before the blasts, only to have the lights around Christina's mirror explode as well. Glittering splinters now protruded from every wall, and Dr. Trug's coat sparkled as though set with rhinestones. Her arms and face were bloodied, but the wounds were superficial, at worst.

There was a bank of lights directly over our seats, she thought, worriedly. She glanced over at Dr. Trug, who was busy listening to someone on his comm set.

"Cat reports your husband is bruised, but safe," he informed her. "And Mr. Archer had an issue with his car, and was therefore outside at the time. But the bad news is, Mr. Géricault, never returned to his seat. He remains unaccounted for."

"Now what do we do?"

"Evacuate."

Christina was standing in the doorway, speaking with the director and a man in overalls -- Carlina guessed him to be a stage hand. Behind them she could hear a cacophony of shouting and screaming, accompanied by a wail of sirens as the medi teams arrived.

"Boros says, the only way out is through the service dock," relayed Christina. "Everything else is blocked off, and there's a whole flock of people leaving from the stage."

"What about the actors' entrance?" Asked Dr. Trug.

"The ceiling's fallen, but it's not too bad," said the stage hand. "But you're not going to get more than one or two through there at a time."

Dr. Trug nodded.

"Meet us at the stage door," he said into the comm.

Holding hands, the two women followed the star-devil out of the dressing room and into the chaos of the backstage corridors. Later, they would learn that the lower balcony had fallen, forcing everyone in the orchestra seating to evacuate through the dressing rooms. Backstage was a river of humanity, as actors and patrons alike pushed their way to the service docks. Meanwhile, a medi team was attempting to go against the current with a motorized gurney. The press of people was suffocating, but somehow, the three of them managed to get across to the narrow passageway leading to the actors' entrance.

"He left us an obvious path for escape," Dr. Trug

explained, as he cleared the rubble. "Which means we can safely assume he'll be waiting there. Mr. Archer, however, will be coming for us here. ... Ladies first!"

Carlina struggled through the rubble, cursing mildly as her dress tore again. Christina had it worse, though, as the dress she wore was very tight fitting. Dr. Trug nearly had to carry her.

"Sheesh! Stupid costume! Why couldn't I be sexy in overalls?"

"Don't worry about it," Carlina said. "We're almost there."

A ceiling support had fallen in the corridor ahead of them, but it only blocked part of the hallway. Beyond that, they could see the door.

"Oh, goat-piddle," Christina muttered, as the heel broke off of her shoe. She hung back a moment in order to remove her footwear, while Carlina continued on, followed by Dr. Trug.

As they moved past the damage, however, she realized someone was standing, very quietly, on the other side of the beam.

"Mr. Géricault!"

"Going somewhere, my dear?"

Immediately, Dr. Trug reached for his gun, but Mr. Géricault already had his at the ready. He gave the star-devil nearly the full clip; shooting him in the shoulder, hip, neck, and knee.

At the sound of gunfire, Christina bolted barefoot back to the dressing rooms. Carlina ran the other way, reaching the door just as the Facilitator caught up with her. He grabbed her around her chest, pulling her against him. She felt something cold and hard press against her side.

"Come along, madame," he said in her ear. "You have an appointment to keep."

"This isn't over, Ger!" Dr. Trug shouted from the hall. "They'll never allow her through the Process!"

"Shut up!"

Mr. Géricault fired off another round in his direction, before pushing Carlina through the door to the rampway outside.

Her heart sank when she saw the Cadillac. Somehow, they had prevented Mr. Archer from reaching the ramp. Still, the driver kept glancing around, as though he expected something to be coming around the corner at any minute. There was hope in that.

"Get in! ... You take care of the car?"

"Sorry, Ger," the driver apologized. "They caught me before I could do anything. We'd better hurry."

Mr. Géricault was about to force her into the back seat, when a block of concrete hit him in the head.

"You will unhand my wife this minute!"

"NIGEL!"

Carlina tried to wrest free, but stopped when Mr. Géricault pressed the gun to her head.

"I suggest you rethink any heroics," he said. "Both of you."

"I told you once before," Nigel replied, quietly advancing along the ramp. "I will not have you take another woman from me."

"And you would stop me how?" Chided Mr. Géricault. "A fistfight? You have no weapon."

"Perhaps."

Nigel pulled a large shard of glass from underneath his blazer (it looked like a piece of theatre lighting) and lunged at the vytoc. He was aiming for the crystal, but Mr. Géricault forced Carlina in front of his chest. The shard slashed his neck, coming very close to her cheek. She felt him move the gun from her head and, without even thinking, she shoved her elbow into Mr. Géricault's groin. Unfortunately, that did not prevent him from firing. Horrified, she watched as Nigel staggered back, his shirt and trousers stained with blood.

Shoving Carlina roughly into the car, Mr. Géricault aimed the gun again, this time at Nigel's head. He pulled the trigger, but the gun just made a series if clicking sounds. He was out of bullets.

"Get us out of here!" He shouted, jumping in beside Carlina.

With a squeal of tyres, the big Cadillac roared down

the ramp and then around to another, which brought them up onto the Bridges. They weaved their way through the pedestrian zone, dodging theatregoers and medi teams; heading for a ramp that would take them to the Periphery.

"Can't you go any faster?" Mr. Géricault demanded.

"You wanna try flying?" The driver shot back. "These roads weren't made for a car this big. It's either go slow or jump, and you won't be finding any loopholes in the law of gravity!"

"Then take the main ramp. We have to get as far as...never mind, here he is. FLOOR IT!"

They merged onto the Periphery just as a sleek, black car came up behind them. Terrified, hopeful, and not quite conscious of what she was doing, Carlina pushed her hands deep between the seat cushions. Much to her surprise, she found a seat belt. She wasted no time belting herself in. They were already doing eighty.

The Firebird kept pace but was still some lengths behind, when they reached level 95. With the entrance to the Black Tower so close, surely, she thought, they'd be stopping soon.

But it wasn't over yet! Instead of slowing down, Mr. Géricault ordered the driver to take evasive action. They turned down the wide concourse of the flat, dodging another selection of pedestrians. This time, it was street sweepers and people returning home from the pubs.

She couldn't bear to look ahead. Instead, she kept her gaze trained on the rear window, hoping she wouldn't see too many bodies left in their wake.

"Please," she cried. "Slow down! You're going to hurt somebody!"

"That happens to be my intention," said Mr. Géricault. "Now, Port!"

Carlina screamed as the car fishtailed sideways, taking the turn too fast. Wildly, they raced down another service ramp and back out onto the Periphery. But the black car was better at turns. It was so close now that she could see Mr. Archer's face through the reflections on the windscreen.

"Slow down! You're going to kill us!"

"Not likely. Damn him! Try another run at 75."

The driver bypassed the flat in favour of the service ramps directly underneath. He took a turn so sharp that Carlina was certain she felt part of the car leave the road. Still, Mr. Archer kept with them.

Another sharp turn found them going up on a "down" ramp. Fortunately, this didn't prove as dangerous as it should have been. There was no traffic trying to go the other way.

"Take the ramp to sixty by tower 7," ordered Mr. Géricault.

"Are you insane? It's closed for maintenance!"

"Well he doesn't know that!"

Carlina wished she could warn Mr. Archer somehow, but nobody had thought to give her a comm set. She could do nothing, but look helplessly out the window as the Cadillac took a ramp that was under repair and barely wide enough for it to fit through. The car bumped and shimmied over the rough surface, finally swinging over to a temporary "detour" ramp.

Again, they were going the wrong way: this time, down on an "up" ramp. Except they weren't alone. Carlina shrieked at the sight of lights approaching.

"Shut up, woman! Take the breakdown lane! NOW!"

In the nick of time, they pulled into an emergency lane just as a large, seven-wheeled van drove past, catching the black car in the narrow curve of the detour ramp.

Thanks to the van's wedge-shaped hood, the Firebird was pushed upward as they collided, forcing it onto the railings. For a moment, it looked as though it would just fall back onto the ramp, but Mr. Archer had been driving far too fast for the guard rails to protect him. For one painful second, the black car teetered on the edge before dipping down, and over, and out of sight.

"Got him!" Mr. Géricault cried, victoriously.

Carlina was crying as well, but they weren't tears of joy. She curled up with her head buried in the seat, her back to Mr. Géricault. In her mind, she could still see the car falling from the ramp. It was interspersed with images of her husband staggering, bleeding, by the stage door.

Mr. Géricault had won the battle. She had no other option but to surrender.

"I want to see my children," she said, softly. "One last time."

"You will see them plenty, " Mr Géricault said, sounding irritated. "I keep trying to tell you! You don't have to leave them! It's the entire *point* of Latebra: humans and vytoc living openly. Families staying together! You will change, but you won't ever have to be separated."

"Still, it's a very big change," she replied. "And I want to see them before...before I do it."

"Then have it arranged," he sighed, handing her his net-phone.

The Cadillac, meanwhile, had slowed to a more respectable speed and was returning again to the Periphery.

"Mr. Cornelius? It's Carlina...yes, I'm all right – physically...Look, I need to see you and the children at the Black Tower...yes, soon as possible...it's a long story. Can I explain later?...Thanks, good-bye."

She shut off the phone, hopeful in that Mr. Cornelius had sounded suspicious. Would there be someone else he could call on to help her? She wondered how many star devils there were. That blonde man -- the one who had been with Dr. Trug at the Underpass – whatever happened to him?

At last, they drove into the parking zone of the Black

Tower. Carlina stared forlornly as they passed the scrap of flag marked with the red devil. It wasn't difficult to guess whose space *that* had been.

Strange. She'd always thought of star-devils as being invincible, somehow. Yet Mr. Géricault had just crippled one and very likely killed another.

"For the love of God, woman! Will you take off your seat belt!"

She was out of the car now and her legs were moving, but everything felt like it was happening to somebody else. Really, it was only the prospect of seeing her children again that kept her moving at all.

She was not expecting to see Mr. Cornelius standing in the vertical; leaning on the destination keypad.

"Going up?"

"My children?" She blurted it out before Mr. Géricault could say a word.

"Children. Level 66. And you sirs?"

"Can the comedy," growled Mr. Géricault. "Just take us to the kids and be quick about it. We've got things to do."

"You're sure about that?" Mr. Cornelius asked, innocently. But Mr. Géricault just glared at him.

The vertical opened up, and Mr. Cornelius led them to a comfortable little suite. Carlina found Robyn and Sophia lying sound asleep on a large bed. Nearby, a nurse sat on a sofa, holding Jonathan, and looking ready to fall asleep herself.

"No, don't get up," she said to her. "We'll just be a minute, and … it might be better if they don't see me go."

"What? You going somewhere?" Mr. Cornelius still had a very innocent look about him, but now she caught the edge to his voice.

"Dr. Trug gave me a heads-up," he whispered. "I was halfway here by the time you called."

"You've dawdled long enough," said Mr. Géricault, testily. "It's time we were going – *now*."

"Good-bye," Carlina said, weakly, touching each child on the cheek. Then, squaring her shoulders, she turned to Mr. Géricault.

"Let's get it over with."

He brought her back into the vertical for the short trip to level 62. Silently, she followed him into the strange, frescoed room that held the portal.

"Achtung!"

Mr. Géricault stopped dead in his tracks.

Standing in front of the portal was the blonde star-devil Carlina remembered from the Underpass. He was wearing an outlandish blue and white uniform and holding the biggest gun she'd ever seen.

Behind her, a voice spoke. And for once, she was very glad Mr. Géricault still had a firm grip on her arm. She about fainted.

"The game is up, Ger," said, Mr. Archer. "You lose."

men! Good show!"

With a wave, he hobbled off in the direction of the stairwell, while the men began hosing away the spilled petrol.

Favouring his leg, Natonoc didn't so much walk down the stairs as slide along on the banisters. Pausing a moment to reset his collarbone, he shimmied across a narrow catwalk and entered the Black Tower at a brisk limp, his broken bones protesting every inch of the way. But there was no time to lose. Portysanon's Cadillac was already in its stall.

Of course, he had no way of knowing about Carlina's last request. Right now, the best he could hope for was that Martynoc would stand his ground and keep her on this side of the portal.

"Himmel, Arsch und Zwirn! What happened to you?" Martynoc exclaimed as Natonoc staggered into the chamber.

"It appears one cannot plea bargain in matters of gravitational law," he said, sliding down along the wall. He came to a rest on the floor, deciding he wasn't going to move further unless it was absolutely necessary. As it was, anyone entering would likely walk right past without noticing him.

"Don't suppose you've seen any action?"

"Not so much as a mouse," Martynoc replied.

"Good."

His P-38 was still snug in its holster and Natonoc took a moment to check the clip.

"Four rounds. Should be enough at this range. How

are you for bullets?"

Martynoc only laughed. He was standing guard cradling an MG44 machine gun, its ammunition belt draping gracefully to a case at his feet.

Fortunately, they didn't have to wait long.

"Achtung!"

Gerysalon barged his way in, with Carlina staggering along beside him. She nearly jumped when Natonoc spoke, shock and amazement vivid on her tear-stained face. Gerysalon just looked angry.

"Stand aside! We have business on the Line!"

"You may go, but the lady must stay behind," Martynoc told him.

"She has given her consent to join," Gerysalon said, playing his trump card. "Is that not right, Doctor?"

Carlina gave Natonoc a pleading look.

"Come now, my dear. Did you or did you not consent?"

A vytasynene addict cannot lie. But, as any lawyer can tell you, the answer you get often depends on how the question is asked.

"Did you consent *under duress?*"

"Yes."

"No farther questions, your Honour," Natonoc grinned.

Martynoc raised the machine gun to the level of

Gerysalon's neck.

"You may pass," he said again. "But not with the lady."

"I'll see you before the Council," Gerysalon growled, letting go of Carlina's arm.

"Das ist mir scheißegal."

For a moment Gerysalon looked as though he might try to fight. Then he thought better of it, pushing past Martynoc to step into the portal.

"Is he gone?" Carlina asked, staring into the blackness.

"Gone from here, anyway," Martynoc told her.

"I just wish I could be sure he was gone for good," she said, wistfully.

"We aim to see that he's as good as gone," Coriolon said from the doorway. "And just to let you know, the boys are back from the theatre. There's drinks and tapioca pudding in the common room, should you care for any."

Carlina's timer answered for her, the shrill alarm making all of them jump.

"Oh, no," she moaned, hitting the reset. "I left my purse in Christina's dressing room!"

"Now don't you worry about a thing," Coriolon assured her. "I brought a vial with the baby things, and I'm sure we can find a syringe around here someplace." He took her by the arm and led her back out into the corridor.

As for Natonoc, he was trying very hard not to fall into a regenerative coma. He knew he needed to rest ... to heal ...and the portal was right there in front of him. He should be going now ...

But that would mean missing the party.

"Think you could give me a lift up?"

With a little help from Martynoc, he made his way down to the common room

"My! Don't *we* look the wrong end of a sausage grinder!"

Kittyvoc, Fosteperon, and Talonyvoc were seated around a table cluttered with bottles which looked as though they had been purloined from Gerysalon's office.

"Name yer poison!" Fosteperon said as Martynoc helped Natonoc into a chair.

"Arsenic."

"I got gin an' tonic."

"That'll do nicely. By the way, Gerysalon owes me a car."

"I'll put that on the list," Kittyvoc said, handing him a drink. "Right after 'new theatre.'"

Despite the fact that he was the only one wearing a military uniform (circa 1812) Martynoc was the only one in the room who *didn't* look as though he'd been through a war. Both Kittyvoc and Fosteperon had been buried in the rubble, and their faces were a patchwork of bruises and lacerations.

Talonyvoc, meanwhile, had fallen into the hands of a medi team, who were clearly inexperienced in regards to vytoc first aide. They had wrapped him up, head to toe, until he was nearly mummified in splints and bandages. He lay on a stretcher, drinking Pilsner through an elaborately twisting straw.

"So," Natonoc asked him. "How was the show?"

Chapter Twenty-Six

"It's certainly been a pleasure having you with us, Dr. White," the physician said, signing the release forms. "It's not every day we see a gastric specialist with an abdominal wound."

"And may it be a long time before you see another," said Nigel, getting into the wheelchair. "And do give my regards to Dr. Pynkson and especially Nurse Lyndahl. I'm sure she's glad to see the last of me."

"It's true, doctors don't always make the best patients. Perhaps we'll meet again under more professional circumstances."

Nigel took his copy of the release form, while an orderly took hold of the wheelchair. A few more final good-bye's, and he was off and heading for the lift.

Out of pure masochism, he looked over the bill. The medi team had brought him to the nearest hospital to the theatre, which happened to be Cloudy Point Medical Center. This was Titan City's signature hospital, so he really couldn't complain, except that it tended to cater to the upper levels and was, therefore, priced accordingly. He would have demanded an immediate transfer to Research, but Carlina had informed him that the Liaison Office would be picking up the charges.

Going home was a most surreal ride, however. Cloudy Point was located on the 150th level of Tower 16, which also housed the Family Health Clinic on level 85. The orderly wheeled Nigel into an express lift, which connected the two medical centres, so that he would be leaving the hospital via the clinic entrance ... in an entirely different neighbourhood. Put into London terms, he was exiting St. Mary's by way of Whitechapel.

Mr. Foster was waiting for him at the Clinic entrance.

"You're certainly looking better than the last time I saw you."

"Fit as the proverbial fiddle," Nigel replied. "Except they've got me on vytoc grub for another week."

"Blood and virgin's tears?"

"More like thin soup, gelatin, and that vile meschel-bean gruel. Don't know how your lot can stand it."

"Meself, I'm still trying to figure out how you know the tears are from a virgin."

"And do you mix them with the blood or serve them on the side as an aperitif?"

"I'm thinking I'll stick to beer," Mr. Foster laughed, ushering Nigel through the door.

It was another hot day, but Mr. Foster was wearing a battered duster over his jade green uniform, which made him look a bit like Dr. Trug. Nigel suspected he was the vytoc Phil so often referred to as "the Australian." However, there was something in the way the man talked, that made him question that assumption.

"You're not really Australian, are you?"

Mr. Foster smiled.

"Might know you'd peg me for a pom," he said. "But yer right. I'm from the Midlands, originally. Went to Birmingham for what I thought was a proper job, and won meself six years transportation. That's six years, mind, only if you can find the means for getting home again. Took nearly fifteen years, but I found me a way out eventually." He tapped the crystal at his throat.

"Was it worth it?"

"For me? Yeah. The Process isn't for everyone, of course -- gotta give up pies for one. But every choice has its downside. It all comes down to what's important; what yer willing to live without."

"Suppose."

They were crossing over to the wide bridge connecting Tower 22 with the rest of the flat. Nigel glanced down over the railings to the rampways below, trying not to imagine a black car plunging into the abyss.

"I do hope Mr. Archer is feeling better."

"Nat's still got about a month of regen ahead of 'em," Mr. Foster said. "But he should be out by Christmas."

"Good to hear. ... Oh, dear God! What are *they* doing here?"

Coming up on his apartment block, Nigel could see a crowd of people milling around the front entrance. Many of them looked to be newspeople.

"Been chasing them from the house ever since the theatre went kablooie," Mr. Foster admitted. "But, no matter, we can get through this." He pulled a pair of dark glasses from his coat pocket. "Come on, everyone! Stand aside! Nothin' to see here!"

Of course, he should have seen this coming. Lying in hospital, he'd had plenty of time to watch as Titan's new media played the theatre disaster for all it was worth. Somehow, they had found out about his confrontation with Mr. Géricault and (with few facts at their disposal) the story had taken on a life all its own. Nigel was being hailed as a Resistance hero, with one rumour going so far as to declare him the actual leader.

A pity Phil wasn't around to hear *that* one!

Ignoring the shouts from the newspeople, Nigel hurried inside as fast as he could. Fortunately, Mr. Foster's star-devil disguise was doing a good job of parting the crowd.

"I'm beginning to see why Carlina didn't come along with you," he said.

One short ride in the lift and, at long last, Nigel was walking down the familiar corridor leading to his apartment. He put his ear to the door, listening.

"Expecting trouble, Doctor?"

"Worse. A party."

But aside from a banner with WELLCOM HOME

DADI written in crayon, everything appeared refreshingly un-festive. Carlina and Christina were seated around the sofa table with Mr. Cornelius, who was busy passing around a collection of battered photographs. An assortment of pamphlets and paperwork lay on the table as well.

Had it really been ten years since he faced a similar pile of brochures in the Black Tower's infirmary? And now, after all this time, he was going home ... but without Phil.

He clutched his side as he brushed away the tears. The wound wasn't actually hurting him, but it made for a handy excuse.

"DADDY'S HOME!! DADDEEEEEE!"

Three small figures were rapidly converging on his legs.

"Be gentle, loves. Daddy's not quite a hundred per cent yet."

"I'll take any per cent I can," Carlina said, coming over to give him a kiss. "Mr. Cornelius brought over some pictures of the house."

"And it's snurgin' huge!" Christina exclaimed from the sofa. "The kids are gonna get their own rooms. The lucky little rats."

She grabbed Robyn as he ran past and tickled his stomach. The boy shrieked with laughter.

Nigel came over to sit beside her on the sofa. He frowned at the photographs.

"I thought we were supposed to be inconspicuous."

"Come on! Nobody's gonna look for you in a house that ugly," Christina cracked.

"What? You're not coming with us?"

She shook her head.

"Sis and I've been talking and I've decided to stay put," she said. "After all, Mr. Archer says we can't draw attention to ourselves over there. Kinda kills any hope of an acting career, ya know!"

"Besides," Carlina added. "Someone needs to stay and look after Mother."

"As soon as he's put back together," Mr. Cornelius said, changing the subject. "Mr. Archer will begin scouting job prospects for you. Give us a few months to finish getting the house in order, and we should have you back in England by the time the rain lets up."

Nigel noticed the selection of passports among the pamphlets.

"We're Canadian now?"

"Nat thought it best that you be returning from somewhere. After all, things have changed in the last ten years. They've decimalized the currency, for one," explained Mr. Cornelius. "And, should our friend Géricault start asking questions, well, we'd like him to believe you're somewhere in North America."

"You might have to re-do them," Nigel said, reading

his. "They've got the name as Manning."

"Because Dr. White disappeared about a decade ago and certain authorities have not forgotten. I fear Interpol would *very* much like to know what happened to you, and *we'd* prefer that they stay in the dark," Mr. Cornelius grinned. "We figured 'Manning' would be the best alternative, considering your wife's condition."

"I can say it's my name," Carlina explained. "I just won't mention it's my *maiden* name."

"Fair enough."

Nigel picked up a tourist souvenir booklet touting all the things to see and do in Manchester. He'd already been warned about London. If he was to live again in England, he would have to avoid the city of his birth, as well as his family and old friends ... and Janice.

Every decision has its downside.

Flipping through the guide book, he noticed that his arm had suddenly grown an appendage.

"Izzat where we're gonna live?" It asked.

"Yes, Robbie," Nigel answered, giving his son a half-hug. "That's going to be our new home."

Epilogue:

"So, this is it, is it?"

Nigel looked around the marble hall, taking in the graceful curve of the grand staircase and the play of light from the stained glass over the main doors. Above him hung an immense chandelier -- with all it's wiring exposed. Clearly, it predated the light bulb.

"Look! See, it's all right," crooned Mr. Archer from the cellar stairs. He came down the hall, holding Jonathan and speaking in the ridiculous sing-song of someone trying to sooth a frightened child. "Look at the window! See the pretty bluebirds!"

"Boo-burbs?"

"That's right! Bluebirds!"

He set the boy down and Jonathan toddled over to where the images from the stained glass were projected onto the marble flooring. Soon, he was skipping about, happily stomping on the bluebirds.

"Well, Doctor ... what do you think?"

"I think I never want to go through another portal for as long as I live," Nigel said, opening the front doors. Outside was the most perfect spring day a man could ask for. He stood a moment with the warm sun on his face; a cool breeze playing through his hair.

"Is that England?" Asked Robyn, appearing at the threshold.

"It's a small part of England," Nigel answered with a smile. "Come on out! The weather's beautiful."

Hesitantly, Robyn came out onto the porch to stand beside his father. He looked around for a moment and then up ... *way* up.

He turned and ran back inside.

"There might be some adjustments to be had," said Mr. Archer with a smile.

They came back inside to find Sophia had joined Jonathan in the hallway kaleidoscope, while Carlina was exploring the library. Robyn, meanwhile, was in the process of running upstairs.

"Hey, Archie! Where's my room?"

"Go down the long hall to your left," Mr. Archer told him. "There are six bedrooms. Take your pick."

"Top floor!"

"The master bedroom is to the immediate left from the stairway," he added to Nigel. "I should warn you, however, while the rooms in the North Wing are perfectly comfortable most seasons of the year, the central heating only extends to the newer sections of the house. It could get chilly come winter."

"I'm sure we'll think of something by then," Nigel said. "I see you've amassed quite a collection of journals."

"Thought you'd might like to catch up a little." Mr. Archer started to say something else, but the words were drowned out in a horrible cacophony of discordant pounding coming from the parlour.

"We have a piano?" Carlina said, in amazement.

"Or a musically inclined poltergeist," Nigel suggested, as they crossed the hall.

Jonathan was seated before a white baby grand, back straight, his hands moving in graceful arcs as he pounded the keys.

"Admittedly, he does look the part," noted Mr. Archer as Carlina pulled the would-be pianist from his instrument. "He won't want to hear it, but I have a list of local piano teachers in that envelope there on the music rack."

"Mr. Archie!" Shouted Robyn from the top of the stairs. "There's something big running around the flat outside. Is it a bear?"

"No, no, just a dog," Mr. Archer shouted back. "He's very friendly. Why don't you go out and meet him?"

"A dog! Penthouse!"

"No, Robyn! Don't slide..." But Nigel's warning came too late. The boy had already figured out the fastest way to go down a staircase, particularly one possessing a smooth, wide bannister. In seconds, he was running down the hall to the back door.

"He didn't leave it *open*, did he?"

Ever the mother, Carlina started down the hall to close the offending door. She didn't get far before she met up with something large and hairy coming from the other direction.

With a startled scream, she flattened herself against the wall, while the younger children hid themselves behind Mr. Archer's legs.

"Good God, Archer!" Nigel cried, pushing back against a wall of furry exuberance that was trying to lick his face. "You got us the hound of the Baskerville's!"

"Sit, Fluffy!"

At Mr. Archer's command, the dog sat back on its haunches. Robyn came up to scratch it on the head. He was nearly the same height as the dog.

"Are all the animals here this big?" Carlina asked, staring at the creature, wide-eyed.

"Now, I don't mind a dog," Nigel added. "But really, Archer! A Newfoundland?"

"You don't mean to tell me, you never plan to take the children to the seaside?" Exclaimed Mr. Archer.

"Well, of course I will, but..."

"And there *is* a duck pond in the garden."

"Yes, but still..."

"Can your children swim?"

Nigel fell silent. He looked at the Newfoundland.

"Didn't miss a thing, did you?"

"Can we keep him?" Robyn pleaded.

"Yes, we'll keep him," Nigel sighed. "But how about you take him back out into the garden."

"All right! C'mon, Archie!"

"Archie?" Nigel looked bemused.

"A very fine name if I say so myself," grinned Mr. Archer as the younger children tentatively followed Robyn and the dog outside. "Now, you'll find the kitchen is this way. We can put the kettle on and I can introduce you to the fine art of serving tea and biscuits."

As Carlina followed Mr. Archer into the kitchen, Nigel picked out a journal from the library. He could expect to face some adjustment as well. After all, he had a whole decade of research to catch up on. Coming out into the garden, he settled himself into a lawn chair and began reading. Around him, the roses bloomed, a pair of swans floated on the pond, and the children raced about, playing a raucous game of tag with their new friend.

"Can we stay here for ever and ever and ever?" Robyn cried as he blurred past.

"Don't mind if we do," said Nigel.

Acknowledgements:

No book gets written in a vacuum (too hard to breathe, for one thing) and this one owes a great debt to Cy, Terri, Chris Baty, and all the other crazy people involved with the National Novel Writing Month. Without their inspired insanity, this story would have never seen paper.

For medical research, I wish to thank Dr. Paul Uhlig, as well as Dawn McInnis, and the University of Kansas Medical School for the use of their library.

And an enthusiastic shout-out to my friend, Kay, for help with the cover and to the Arney family for giving my early drafts a read, as well as providing plenty of tea, sympathy, and soccer games that make the struggle bearable.

About the Author

Johanna Gedraitis lives mostly in her head, the rest of her life being rather dull and ordinary. When she's not hiding out in a museum somewhere, she resides with her two house-rabbits in the old frontier town of Possum Trot, Missouri.